THE FIVE AND
THE PINK PEAR

THE FIVE are Julian, Dick,
George (Georgina by rights), Anne and
Timmy the dog.

When George's mother buys an antique
chair at an auction, the Five don't expect it
to be the start on an intriguing new
adventure.

Very soon, however, they discover the
chair's valuable secret; and when someone
breaks into their house in the middle of the
night, it becomes clear that another person
knows that secret too. The Five have to do
some dangerous detective work to discover
just *who* this 'mystery man' is and prevent
him from stealing what isn't rightfully
his . . .

Cover illustration by Peter Mennim

The Five and the Pink Pearls

Claude Voilier
translated by Anthea Bell

Hodder
Children's
Books

a division of Hodder Headline plc

British Library C.I.P.

Voilier, Claude
  The Five and the pink pearls.
  I. Title   II. Harvey, Bob   III. Les Cinq se mettent en
  quatre en France. *English*
  843'.914 [J]   PZ7
          ISBN 0 340 60335 6

Typeset by Hewer Text Composition Services, Edinburgh
Printed and bound in Great Britain by
Cox & Wyman Ltd, Reading, Berkshire

Hodder Children's Books
a division of Hodder Headline plc
338 Euston Road
London NW1 3BH

Contents

Going Away for the Holidays

'Oh, *George*,' Aunt Fanny told her daughter, 'I do wish you wouldn't get underfoot like that! It really is getting me down. I could do the packing much better if you'd leave me alone.'

'Well, it's not the sort of weather for going out of doors, is it?' said George, rather crossly. 'It's pouring with rain outside. You can't even see the sea from my bedroom window, there's such a thick mist, let alone look across to Kirrin Island. I'm bored!'

'It's the sort of weather one expects at this time of year,' said Aunt Fanny. 'I'm quite surprised at you, George! Bored, on the first day of the Christmas holidays?'

The word 'holidays' certainly brought a smile back to George's face! It was a face that looked rather like a boy's – and as she kept her hair cut short too, people often thought she really *was* a boy called George, and not a girl who had been christened Georgina! George didn't mind a bit, and hated being called by her real name. She would rather have been a boy, like her cousins Julian and Dick. Not that being a girl had ever stopped her having just as exciting a time as they did.

'You're right, I shouldn't complain of being bored now it's the holidays,' she agreed with Aunt Fanny. 'And what interesting Christmas holidays they're going to be! I know Father's always going away to his scientific conferences and so on – but I never guessed he was going to take *us* with him this time as well. And Julian and Dick and Anne too. What an adventure! You did say it wouldn't be so wet down in the south of the country, didn't you?'

'Well, you can never be sure of that, with our English climate!' said Aunt Fanny, smiling, 'but we certainly do get some particularly wild wintry weather on the coast near Kirrin. I shall be quite glad to go away for a winter holiday, just for a change.' She gently pushed George towards the doorway. 'Off you go, George, there's a good girl – let me get on with the packing, and take Timmy with you. He's no help at all!'

Wherever George went, Timmy went too. She thought he was the best, cleverest dog in the whole world. George and her cousins liked to call themselves the Five – dear old Timmy was the fifth of them, and he shared all their adventures.

'Come on, Timmy!' George told him. 'We're not wanted here! Let's go down to the kitchen and see if we can find something nice to eat to cheer us up!'

They were lucky – they found Joan from the village in the kitchen. Joan had come up to help in the house that day, because Aunt Fanny was so busy packing, and she was just doing some baking.

'Why, there you are, George!' said Joan. 'And you too, Timmy. Now why would *you* be coming to see old Joan? Cupboard love, I'll be bound! Well, just you wait while I finish making the pastry for this apple pie, and I'll see what I can find to keep you two going!'

'I can smell something delicious in the oven!' said George hopefully, and soon she was sitting at the kitchen table with a big mug of steaming hot cocoa and a plate of sultana buns which Joan had just turned out of their baking tray. Timmy wasn't forgotten either – there was a nice juicy bone for him!

'My, what an appetite you do have when you get home for the holidays!' said Joan, smiling as she watched George enjoying the buns. 'Don't they feed you at that school of yours?'

'Well – they *do*,' said George, 'but school food is nothing like yours. I think you're the best cook in the whole world, Joan, and so do Julian and Dick *and* Anne.'

'I must see what I can make for them when they arrive tomorrow, then!' said Joan with a chuckle.

'That'd be lovely, Joan,' said George. 'Of course,

you won't be seeing very much of any of us these holidays.'

'No, so I won't,' Joan agreed. 'It all comes of your father being such a clever scientist – just fancy him taking you all away with him to that conference of his!'

'Isn't it exciting?' said George happily. 'Julian and Dick and Anne don't know yet – it's a secret surprise for them when they get here tomorrow. Oh, I hope tomorrow comes soon!'

George's three cousins usually spent the school holidays with Aunt Fanny and Uncle Quentin at Kirrin Cottage – and they thought that was the plan for this time. Aunt Fanny had been keeping the change of plans a surprise. George couldn't wait for the others to arrive, so that she could tell them.

Luckily it had stopped raining next day, and it was beautiful cold, crisp, clear winter weather in Kirrin village – just the right sort of day for the Christmas holidays. Julian, Dick and Anne had caught an early train, and it was only eleven in the morning when they got off the bus which brought them from the railway station to Kirrin Cottage. They ran happily up the garden path to hug George and her parents.

'Hello, Aunt Fanny! Hello, Uncle Quentin!' said Julian politely.

'Hello there, George,' said Dick. 'What fun to be all together for the holidays!'

'Yes, we're the Five again at last!' little Anne, the youngest of the cousins, said happily.

'Woof! Woof!' said Timmy. *He* agreed too.

Feeling almost deafened by all this noise, Uncle Quentin soon went back to his study to get on with some of his important work – and Aunt Fanny left it to George to tell her cousins about the change in their holiday plans.

'I *say*!' said Dick, with a whistle. 'That's very good of Uncle Quentin. This will be a really different sort of holidays for us!'

'Yes, it will,' said Julian, the eldest of the cousins, a tall, fair-haired, very sensible boy. 'I've heard quite a lot about that international conference on space travel, and I thought Uncle Quentin might be going, because some of his new inventions are to help astronauts – but I never dreamed he'd take us too!'

'I'm glad we're going away as well,' said Anne. 'Is Timmy coming too?'

'I should jolly well think so!' said George. 'Father knows I won't go *anywhere* without dear old Timmy! I'd rather die!'

The Five happily raced outside.

'What lovely weather!' said Anne. 'It's almost a shame to go away from dear old Kirrin when it's as fine as this!'

'It probably won't be fine for long,' George reminded her. 'It will be interesting to spend the Christmas holidays in a big city for a change.

We're lucky the schools broke up early this year, or Father might not have thought of taking us – part of his conference is before Christmas, and then the scientists will take a few days off for Christmas itself and start talking again afterwards. We won't be in Father's way, because he'll be so busy with the conference and all the other scientists!'

'In other words, we'll be free to do whatever we like!' said Dick happily.

'Come to think of it, where are we staying, George?' asked Julian.

'Well, not in a hotel, because it's so expensive, and they might not like Timmy in a hotel. But luckily Mother has some cousins who actually live in the city where the conference is taking place, and they're going abroad for a winter holiday themselves, so they're letting us borrow their flat. We'll have the whole place to ourselves.'

'Oh, good! That'll be much nicer than a hotel,' said Julian.

The children were still talking about the holiday ahead of them as they went for a walk by the sea until lunch-time. Joan had cooked them a delicious roast chicken and an apple and mincemeat crumble, and they all had good appetites after a morning of sea air and sunshine.

That afternoon, however, the sun went in, the rain came down again – the children couldn't play out of doors, and once again they decided that

Christmas in all the lively bustle of a big city would make a very nice change!

It was quite a long journey, so they had to set off early next morning. They changed trains in London, and a couple of hours later, they reached the city where the conference was being held. The children, Aunt Fanny and Uncle Quentin – and Timmy too, of course – all piled into a taxi and were driven to the flat they were borrowing from Aunt Fanny's cousins.

The flat overlooked a busy street – quite a change from the quiet countryside round Kirrin Cottage. It was a big flat, too, with several rooms opening off a passage down the middle of it. The bedrooms faced east and the other rooms faced west.

The four children thought it was a lovely flat – very comfortable, with beautiful furniture. Obviously Aunt Fanny's cousins were rather well off. Timmy seemed to realize he was in somebody else's home and mustn't knock things over. He was walking round exploring, stepping very delicately. Timmy knew the difference between the gravel paths in the garden of Kirrin Cottage and the thick carpet of a flat in a big city.

When the children had unpacked, they went to find Aunt Fanny, who had just finished putting her own things away. 'Now, the first thing is to go and buy food,' she said. 'And it will give us a chance to explore the town too. So while Uncle Quentin's

busy getting down to work, I suggest the rest of us
go out.'

That suited the Five down to the ground. After
their long train journey, they all wanted to stretch
their legs – or in Timmy's case, his paws. They
happily set off.

'I say, this is a change from Kirrin and no
mistake!' said Julian. 'All the buses, and such
crowds of people.'

Aunt Fanny and the Five explored the shops, the
nearby streets, and the big square which was not far
away and had a garden in the middle where you
could play games. They wrote down the numbers
of the buses which went to different parts of the
city. Then the children helped Aunt Fanny to carry
her shopping back to the flat, and Anne helped her
aunt make the supper too – Cousin Jane had a lovely
modern kitchen, with all the latest gadgets.

After supper, Uncle Quentin explained that he
would be out every day while the conference was
on, from quite early in the morning, and wouldn't
be back until it was time for their evening meal.

'Well, I'm sure there will be plenty for the
children and me to do, Quentin dear!' Aunt Fanny
told him. 'Cousin Jane said there are all sorts of
interesting places to visit in this city – and I
believe it's well known as a centre of the antiques
business too, so I shall enjoy going to some of
the auction sales. I do like finding things at a
sale!'

The children grinned – they knew all about Aunt Fanny's passion for going to auctions of antiques and second-hand furniture. And some of the things she had picked up for a song were really very pretty. George could understand how her mother felt, but she hoped Aunt Fanny wouldn't expect the children to trail round the sales with her all the time. They could go about on their own, just as they liked, in the quiet country around Kirrin – surely they wouldn't be expected to have a grown-up with them at every moment, here in the city?

Next morning, at breakfast, George thought she had better get that quite clear. 'Mother,' she said, finishing a last piece of toast and strawberry jam, 'you'll let us go out alone once we know our way round, won't you?'

Aunt Fanny smiled. 'Yes, of course, dear!' she said. 'I'm sure you'll all promise to be sensible, and careful – and I know I can trust you to keep an eye on the others, Julian! You're such a responsible boy for your age.'

'Oh – well, thanks, Aunt Fanny!' said Julian, rather embarrassed by this compliment.

'I'm afraid your cousin George would often get into trouble without you,' added Aunt Fanny.

Well, really! George didn't know whether to laugh or be indignant. It was true that Julian *was* very sensible – but *she* was the one who had often solved a mystery when the Five had one of their exciting adventures. And this big, bustling city seemed just the place for another one . . . could there by any chance be an adventure in store for them these holidays?

An Auction Sale

For the first day or so, the Five and Aunt Fanny went round again, exploring the city and finishing their Christmas shopping. Luckily there were plenty of places in Cousin Jane's flat where they could hide the presents they were going to give each other on Christmas Day. Then, one morning, Aunt Fanny told the children, 'There's a Disney film on at the cinema just down the road – would you like to go and see it this afternoon? I want to go to the sale-rooms in the middle of town myself, to look at the things which are going to be auctioned tomorrow. You don't need to come with me if you think you'll be bored.'

That was nice of Aunt Fanny – but George thought she *would* like to go with her mother. She wouldn't have minded seeing the film, but the trouble was that she couldn't take Timmy to the cinema with her. 'If you don't mind, I'd rather go with you, Mother!' she said, quickly. 'Actually, I find those sales quite interesting myself.'

'So do I,' said Julian. 'I'd like to come as well.'

'I would too,' said Anne, who usually agreed with her big brother.

'Well, of course you can come if you like,' Aunt Fanny told them. 'Apparently it's going to be a sale of the contents of an old lady's house. She died quite recently – she was called Miss Jean Longfield, and she had no family to leave her things to. I've heard that there are a great many nice things in the sale, just the sort I like – old pieces of furniture and unusual, valuable curios and knick-knacks. They're on view at the sale-rooms today, and anyone who's interested in antiques can go and look at them.'

Aunt Fanny and the Five set off that afternoon, in a taxi. The sale-rooms were at the other end of town, and room number 8, where the viewing was being held, was already full of people looking at the furniture and other things on display. Some of the smaller items must have been very valuable, because they were in glass cases, and there were attendants keeping watch on the people who came and went.

The glass cases were quite near the doorway. They contained beautiful Dresden china ornaments, little bronzes, and lovely jade and ivory carvings. Aunt Fanny and the children stood and admired them for some time – even Dick could see that they were very pretty as well as being precious. Then they moved on to look at the furniture. Aunt Fanny wasn't really interested in the bigger pieces of furniture, but she stopped for a long look at a little armchair.

'That's a shape they call a tub chair,' she told the children. 'What a beautiful example!'

'Isn't it pretty?' said Anne.

'It looks quite comfortable, too!' said Dick, and the others laughed. He had a reputation for being rather lazy!

Timmy was such a well-behaved dog that the attendants had allowed him into the viewing room with the others. He seemed to agree with Dick – he was looking at the chair in an appreciative way, just as if he were saying, '*That* would be a good place for a dog to curl up and go to sleep!' George couldn't help laughing.

'Are you thinking of bidding for that chair?' she asked her mother.

'Well, it would look rather nice in the sitting-room at Kirrin, don't you think, children?' said Aunt Fanny.

'Yes, it would,' Julian agreed.

'I *might* try bidding for it tomorrow, if the price doesn't go too high,' Aunt Fanny decided.

She would have liked a closer look at the little chair, but somebody else, a man who had already been looking at it when Aunt Fanny and the children arrived, didn't seem to be in any hurry to move away. He was standing in front of the chair, feeling its upholstery – it was covered with velvet which was rather faded, but otherwise in good condition

– running his fingers over the wooden ribs inside it, looking closely at its back and its feet. Finally, and rather reluctantly, he went away and let Aunt Fanny see the chair at close quarters too.

'He didn't look very nice, did he?' George said to her cousins, under her breath. She had been examining the man while *he* examined the chair. 'I'm afraid he'll be competing with Mother in the bidding if he comes to the sale tomorrow. He seemed rather keen on the chair himself.'

George's fears turned out to be well founded. When Aunt Fanny and the children arrived at the sale-rooms for the Longfield sale next day, George and her cousins recognized the same man among the crowd of people present.

'There! I was right!' George whispered to Dick. 'Our friend of the tub chair is back!'

'He's a bit tubby himself!' said Dick, laughing. 'Got a face like a frog, too!'

Anne had to stifle her giggles. It was quite true – the man *did* look like a frog, with a wide, thin-lipped mouth and big goggle-eyes.

The sale began, and several of the pieces of furniture were bought for quite high prices. Then two assistants brought in the chair Aunt Fanny liked and put it down where everyone could see it. The auctioneer began the bidding, which started at thirty pounds.

'Forty!' called someone.

'Forty-five!'

'Fifty!'

The bidding went on rising, because it was a very pretty little chair. However, once the bids went past seventy-five pounds, everyone dropped out except for Aunt Fanny and 'Frog-face', as the children called him to themselves.

'Eighty!' said the man.

'Ninety!' said Aunt Fanny.

'Ninety-five!'

'A hundred!'

The children knew that Aunt Fanny wasn't going to bid any more than a hundred pounds – that was a lot of money anyway, and she and Uncle Quentin had decided, the night before, that the chair was worth it, but she wouldn't go any higher. However, it looked as if Frog-face had a sudden fit of coughing which meant he couldn't say anything. The children felt more hopeful. The auctioneer raised his hammer.

'A hundred pounds! Going at one hundred pounds . . . going . . . going . . .'

George and her cousins knew that when the auctioneer said 'Gone!' and brought his hammer down, the bidding would be over and the chair would belong to Aunt Fanny.

But at the last moment Frog-face, though unable to speak, began to raise his hand instead. That meant the same as a higher bid – he was going to get the chair after all. However, danger was

averted just in the nick of time! A movement in
the audience made Dick lose his balance, and he
automatically steadied himself by hanging on to
the arm of his nearest neighbour – Frog-face!
Frog-face couldn't finish raising his hand – and
the auctioneer's hammer fell.

The tub chair went to Aunt Fanny! She was
delighted to have bought the pretty piece of furniture.

'She wouldn't have got it but for me!' said Dick to
the others, grinning. 'What luck I was pushed into
that nasty little man just at the vital moment!'

'You didn't hang on to his arm on purpose, I
hope?' said Julian, a little suspiciously.

'Of course not!' said Dick, and he added in a
very virtuous tone of voice, 'That would have been
dishonest, wouldn't it?'

'Yes, it would,' said Julian rather sternly, and
George thought she'd better step in and make peace
between her two cousins.

'I'm sure it was just chance,' she said, 'and anyway, everything's turned out all right, hasn't it?'

Anne was very pleased to see that Aunt Fanny
had got her chair. She was happily paying the money
for it as the children talked. But if Aunt Fanny was
happy, Frog-face certainly wasn't. Aunt Fanny was
telling the sale-room assistants where to deliver the
chair – Flat 3, number 16 Lime Avenue – when
Frog-face came up to her with a forced smile.

'I'm sorry to trouble you, madam,' he began, 'but

I really did very much want to buy the chair you've just been bidding for. It's most important to me. May I ask if you would be good enough to sell it to me? At well above the price you've just paid, of course!'

Aunt Fanny looked at the man. He was very well dressed, and spoke perfectly politely – but all the same there was what sounded like the suggestion of a threat in his words, and he seemed quite sure she *would* sell the chair to him. Aunt Fanny didn't like his attitude at all.

'Well, I'm very sorry,' she said coldly, 'but I very much wanted to buy the chair myself, so I'm keeping it!'

The man tried to argue with her, but she cut him short – people standing near them wanted silence so that they could hear the bidding for the next item in the sale. Frog-face strode angrily towards the doorway.

'Gosh, it's lucky he didn't notice me properly!' muttered Dick. 'After I made him miss his bid – and honestly, Julian, that really *was* an accident – I ducked under his arm so as to make my way over to you others, and he hardly had time to see me. I think it was just as well!'

Aunt Fanny and the children stayed to watch a little more of the sale – and Aunt Fanny was tempted into bidding for another piece of furniture she hadn't noticed the day before, although it too was in the sale of the contents of Miss Longfield's house. This one was a very attractive little writing-desk which she bought quite cheaply. The saleroom staff said it would be delivered next day, at the same time as the tub chair. When they left for Kirrin, Aunt Fanny told the children, she would have both pieces of furniture sent on by road.

By now Timmy had had enough of standing quietly in all this crowd – *he* wasn't interested in the bidding, and couldn't even see what was going on! So Aunt Fanny and the children rewarded him for being a good dog by taking him for a walk. Aunt Fanny was very pleased with her two purchases, and was looking forward to their delivery next day. Julian, Dick and Anne were pleased that *she* was pleased. But there was something about it all that bothered George.

'I wonder why Frog-face was so very keen to buy that chair?' she asked herself. 'He was willing to pay more than it was worth, too. . . yes, that was really very odd!'

The tub chair and the little desk were delivered late next morning. While Aunt Fanny tipped the men who had brought them, George and her cousins carefully carried both pieces of furniture into the sitting-room, which was bathed in the bright sun-light of a crisp December day, to have a good look at them and then brush and polish them nicely.

No sooner had Aunt Fanny closed the door after the delivery men, however, than the doorbell rang again. She was surprised, because she wasn't expecting anyone else. However, she opened the door once more.

And there on the mat stood Frog-face! The man who had been bidding against her for the tub chair the day before! Aunt Fanny was going to say something, but Frog-face, once again sounding most polite about it, got in first.

'Now, madam, please don't throw me out before you've heard what I have to say! I have a most important reason for troubling you. Believe me, I'm most apologetic!'

Aunt Fanny wasn't quite sure what to say, so she let him into the hall, and stood waiting to hear his explanation. He began by introducing himself.

'My name is Ernest Parry, and I have a shop selling curios and souvenirs. It's in Mimosa Avenue. That tub chair you bought yesterday is a piece of furniture I've been wanting for a long time . . . it belonged to an old lady who was a dear friend of mine. I've often admired it in her sitting-room. But now my dear old friend is dead, and I thought that as a memento of her, I'd like to buy the chair where I so often used to see her sitting.'

This pathetic story would have sounded more likely if Aunt Fanny's visitor hadn't looked and sounded quite so oily.

'I'm so sorry,' said Aunt Fanny, rather coldly, 'but I like the chair very much myself, and I want to keep it. That's why I bought it! Surely you could have chosen some other memento from Miss Longfield's things?'

'Unfortunately I was *particularly* fond of that chair . . . it's a matter of its sentimental value! Now, do at least let me make you a very good offer for it! Shall we say a hundred and fifty pounds?'

Aunt Fanny was getting really annoyed by Mr Parry's insistence. She didn't like him at all, and she told him it was no good, even if he doubled his offer.

'It's not a question of money,' she said firmly. I'm keeping my chair, so let's forget about all this, shall we?'

George had just been about to cross the hall and go into the kitchen in search of a brush for the antiques, when Mr Parry rang the bell – so she stood where she was, just inside the sitting-room door where she couldn't be seen, listening to his brief conversation with Aunt Fanny. Her cousins came tiptoeing over to join her.

They saw Aunt Fanny showing her uninvited visitor out again. As soon as the door was safely closed behind him, George came out into the hall.

'Well, he certainly had a cheek!' she told her mother. 'Fancy following you here to try and buy that chair back!'

'I suppose he must have heard me giving this address at the sale-rooms yesterday,' said Aunt Fanny, sounding rather cross.

'And then he waited for the delivery man to arrive,' said Dick.

'He seems to think an awful lot of that tub chair,' said Julian. 'It's a pretty chair, I agree, but still!'

George frowned. 'I don't know that that's the only reason for the way he's carrying on. There must be something else . . . after all, it isn't such a rare, valuable chair as all that! And he was obviously lying when he said it had sentimental value for him. Just as Mother said, he could easily have chosen something else in the sale as a memento.'

'George the sleuth on the trail again!' said Dick, laughing. 'You smell something fishy, do you?'

'Yes, I do,' said George, quite seriously. 'I don't like that frog-faced man at all. And what's more, if I hadn't smelt something fishy on certain *other* occasions, there are a lot of exciting adventures we'd never, ever have had, so there, Dick!'

Aunt Fanny, who had been into the kitchen, came back with a brush and a little vacuum cleaner. 'Now then, children, to work!' she said cheerfully. 'I'll leave you to look after my two new purchases while I make us some lunch.'

The Five went back into the sitting-room, and set to work on the two antiques. Dick and Julian had decided to tackle the desk. They went over it with a duster, and then started to polish it up. There was a good deal of carved woodwork, so this was quite a job.

Meanwhile, Anne gently but firmly brushed the

faded velvet upholstery of the tub chair. She knew just the way to treat a delicate piece of furniture, and George, who was much clumsier than her cousin, was happy to stand and watch! Timmy sat warming himself in the sunlight, enjoying being with his mistress and her cousins – he was so fond of all the children!

'The seat itself isn't too dusty,' said Anne, brushing away.

'If what Frog-face said was true, the old lady probably sat in it every day,' said George. 'I expect she took good care of it.'

'The most difficult bit to clean is where the seat joins the back, and down at the bottom of the arms,' Anne went on. 'That's where the dust usually collects.'

As she spoke, the little girl had put her hand down into the space behind the back of the seat. Suddenly she uttered an exclamation.

'Oh, George! I can feel something. It must have slipped down the back of the seat by accident. No, it can't have done – it's too big for that. Someone must have put it there on purpose.'

George craned over to have a look. 'What sort of a thing is it?' she asked. 'Can't you get it out? Hurry up, do!'

Anne groped about a little longer, and then, with some difficulty, pulled her find out from the back of the chair. It was a flat, oval, pale blue box.

'Looks like a jewellery box,' said George. 'Here, let's see!'

Julian and Dick, abandoning the desk, had come over to the two girls.

'Quick, George, open it,' said Dick.

George lifted the lid of the box – and all four cousins exclaimed in amazement.

'Pearls!' cried Anne.

'What a magnificent necklace!' said Julian. 'Look how many pearls there are!'

'Do you think they're *real*?' breathed Dick.

'They *look* real,' said George. 'At least, I think so. Let's go and show them to my mother!'

The children dashed into the kitchen, with Timmy at their heels.

'Mother, Mother!' cried George. 'Look what we found down the back of the old chair!'

— 3 —

The Pink Pearls

Aunt Fanny stood there running the pearl necklace through her fingers over and over again. She was astonished! It consisted of two rows of pearls, the most beautiful pale pink in colour.

'These pearls look to me as if they have a really wonderful lustre, I think they *must* be real,' she said. 'But I'm no expert – I don't know for sure. I think we'd better put this necklace safely away for the time being, and find out about it later.'

'If they *are* real pearls, they must be very valuable, mustn't they?' asked George.

'Yes, very valuable indeed,' said Aunt Fanny.

'Do they belong to you?'

'Well . . . I suppose so. Seeing that I bought the tub chair, and old Miss Longfield died without having any family to inherit her things.'

'Oh, I'm so pleased for you, Aunt Fanny!' cried Anne.

But George had other things on her mind besides the fortune which so unexpectedly seemed to have come her mother's way.

'Do you know what I think?' she cried excitedly.

'Not till you tell us, George!' said Julian.

'Well, I *will* tell you. I bet you Timmy to a bunch of bananas that frog-faced man – Mr Parry, I mean – knew those pink pearls were down the back of the tub chair. And he was so keen to buy the chair himself because he wanted to get hold of them!'

This time Dick was impressed by his cousin's detective abilities. She had often had brainwaves like this before – and her cousins all knew it. Aunt Fanny thought much the same as George did, too.

'You may be right, George,' she said. 'But we can't prove it.'

'Frog-face doesn't look honest to me!' said Dick wisely.

'You mustn't judge people by appearances. Anyway, I refused his offer, and I was quite right too! Let's forget about him and put those pearls away and – oh, my goodness, the potatoes are boiling over!'

Aunt Fanny ran to the kitchen stove, and the children went back into the sitting-room, but though they were soon brushing and polishing the chair and desk again, they could think of nothing but the pink pearls.

'What a funny thing to do – putting them down the back of a chair like that!' said Julian, polishing the desk.

'Yes, it was a strange place to hide them,' Dick agreed.

George was busy exploring every inch of the rest of the old chair, just in case it contained any more treasures. But she didn't find anything. However, next moment Dick made another discovery. He had started polishing the little brass knobs on the drawers of the desk. Suddenly he stopped. 'Hallo!' he said, interested. 'There's a tiny little knob here, black, you can hardly see it, which doesn't seem to be for anything.'

Hardly thinking what he was doing, he pressed the knob. He heard a slight click – and then, before his very eyes, a little panel slid aside, showing a secret drawer behind it.

'I say – a secret hiding place!' cried Dick, delighted. 'Terrific! I wonder if there's a wallet full of banknotes inside?'

George and Anne came rushing over to the boys. 'What? Where? What have you found?' cried George.

Dick was exploring the secret drawer. But he was disappointed. There was no wallet full of money there, and no more jewellery, just a thin, yellowish envelope, very ordinary-looking and not even sealed.

In her impatience, George never even thought of taking the envelope to her mother first! She snatched it from Dick's hands and opened it at once.

Taking out a sheet of paper covered with spidery

writing, she read out loud: 'In this document written by my own hand, I, Jean Longfield of 28 Almond Road, leave my friend Elizabeth Caswell, as a memento of me, the necklace I inherited from my Aunt Flora, consisting of two rows of real pink pearls, ninety-eight pearls in all . . .'

'Ninety-eight!' cried Julian. 'That's the exact number of pearls in the necklace Anne found. I counted them.'

'Two rows of pink pearls – well, that means it *has* to be the same necklace!' added Dick.

'This document was written twenty years ago,' said George, taking another look at the sheet of paper. 'And Miss Longfield died quite recently.'

'Then it's somebody called Elizabeth Caswell who really owns those pink pearls,' said Julian. 'How can we find her, I wonder?'

'Are you sure that sort of will thing is really about the pink pearls I found down the back of the chair?' asked Anne.

'Yes, of course it must be!' said George. 'Remember, both those pieces of furniture came from the sale of Miss Longfield's things. And the old lady's said to have died without making any kind of will – which may be true as the rest of her possessions are concerned. But twenty years ago she decided she wanted to leave one special thing to her friend Elizabeth Caswell – so she wrote down her wish to leave her pearls as the legacy, and I expect that piece of paper has been in the secret drawer ever since, going yellow with time.'

'We'd better show it to Aunt Fanny, hadn't we?' said Dick.

Aunt Fanny was very surprised to read the 'will' about the pearls.

'So I was quite right in thinking that necklace is made of genuine pearls,' she said. 'It must be amazingly valuable.'

The children would all have agreed that Aunt Fanny was the least grasping, most generous person in the world – and she didn't feel at all disappointed to find out that she had no real claim to the pearls herself. She thought quickly.

'I'll go and visit a lawyer this afternoon,' she decided. 'I'll show him this document, and give him the necklace, and ask him to try and find the lady the pearls were left to. I think this Elizabeth Caswell ought to be very grateful to you children for making sure she gets what must be a real little fortune!'

'Oh, Mother, do you really need to go to a lawyer?' said George, suddenly having a bright idea. 'I'm sure we could find the owner of the pearls ourselves. It would be something for us to do – and you know we love being detectives and making inquiries!'

Aunt Fanny smiled. When she thought about it, she decided there wasn't really any need to go to a lawyer, or at least not yet. She did indeed know how the Five liked solving the mysteries that always seemed to come their way – and though they had been so excited at the idea of going away for the holidays, she was afraid they might be bored in a city flat after a while. The two discoveries they had made certainly meant they deserved a bit of fun, thought Aunt Fanny.

'Yes, do let us try to find Elizabeth Caswell ourselves, Aunt Fanny!' Dick begged.

'It would be such an interesting thing to do!' Anne agreed.

'Anne's right,' said Julian, in his serious way. 'And if we *don't* manage to find her, well, there'll still be plenty of time to go to a lawyer, or the police. After all, it only means a few days' delay.'

'And we'd really enjoy trying to track her down!' said George, her eyes shining.

'Very well!' said her mother. 'Since you're all so keen, see what you can do! I just hope you're soon successful – I don't want to keep such a valuable piece of jewellery here for very long. It's a great responsibility.'

'Hurray!' cried George. 'Another little mystery for the Famous Five! Three cheers! Hip, hip, hurray!'

Lunch was eaten very quickly that day. The children helped Aunt Fanny do the washing up, and then they held a council of war. Timmy was there too, of course.

'First of all,' said George, 'the easiest way to try

and find Mrs or Miss Caswell would be to look for her name in the telephone book.'

'Quite right,' said Julian, picking up the big directory. 'Let's see.'

He leafed rapidly through the pages. Leaning over Julian's shoulder, the other three watched his finger going down a long column of names beginning with C.

'Cartwright . . . Carver . . . Casburn . . . Case . . . Cassidy . . . Castle . . . Catchpole . . . bother! No Caswells in this city.'

'Have another look,' suggested Dick.

'There's nothing wrong with my eyes, thanks!' Julian told him. 'See for yourself. Not a single Caswell.'

'Perhaps Elizabeth Caswell isn't on the phone.'

'Or she could be ex-directory – some people are.'

'Or perhaps she's left the city – if she ever lived here.'

'Or maybe she got married and now she's using her husband's name.'

'Or she could be dead, like Miss Longfield.'

'That's quite possible – after all, the "will" was made twenty years ago. All sorts of things could have happened to Miss Longfield's friend since then.'

'But how are we going to find out what?'

'Woof!' said Timmy, helpfully. He probably thought he was making a useful contribution to the council of war.

The children all looked a bit downcast – until George said cheerfully, 'Well, never mind! It would have been almost *too* easy just to find her in the telephone book.'

'It's a pity Miss Longfield didn't think of writing her friend's address down,' said Anne.

Dick dramatically struck his forehead. 'I've had an idea!' he told the others. 'Let's go to the place where Miss Longfield used to live. We do at least know *that* address!'

'Yes, but what earthly good will it do to go and look at it?' asked Anne, puzzled.

'Well, we might meet somebody living near by who knew Miss Longfield well, and then that person might be able to tell us about her other friends – and give us a lead to finding Elizabeth Caswell!'

'That's good thinking, Dick!' said Julian.

'No need to sound so surprised, Ju!' remarked his younger brother. 'Young George isn't the *only* one in this family to get brainwaves, you know!'

George was thinking, and frowning a little. She nodded. 'Yes – it's a good idea,' she agreed. 'The only thing is, how are we going to get there?'

'By bus, of course!' said Dick. 'Or no – there's an underground train system in this city, just like London's, only smaller, so why don't we use that? It's usually quicker to get to places by Tube.'

'Maybe,' George pointed out, 'but if we go by Tube we'll have to lug poor old Timmy about in a basket. And I'm jolly well not leaving him at home!'

Her cousins' faces fell. 'Yes,' said Julian, 'they don't let animals into the Tube stations unless they're in baskets. And Timmy's quite a hefty weight to carry – he hates it, too.'

There was silence while they thought. Then George's face suddenly lit up. 'I know what!' she said. 'We *will* put Timmy in a carrier – but we won't carry him!'

'Is that a riddle, or what?' asked Dick.

'You wait and see. I'm sure my idea will work. Just give me a few minutes, and then we'll start out.'

She went off, followed by Timmy, and leaving her cousins wondering what on earth she was up to. A moment later she was back in triumph, carrying a big, floppy wicker shopping basket. Timmy was still trotting after her.

'Right, off we go!' she said. 'Let's go and find where Miss Jean Longfield used to live.'

The Five set off for the nearest Tube station – they had already looked at a street map of the city, and found out that Almond Road, where Miss Longfield had lived, was on the other side of town.

'We'll have to change trains half-way,' said Julian. 'And I suppose that'll mean carrying old Timmy for miles and miles along a corridor!'

'Don't worry, Ju!' said George, smiling. 'I told you I'd found a way to make Timmy take the weight himself!'

Sure enough, as soon as they reached the station, George held the basket open, and Timmy obediently jumped into it. George and Dick each took a handle of the basket. They stopped as soon as they had reached the steps going down to the platforms, where they were out of the ticket clerk's sight, and George told her dog, 'Right, you can walk now, old chap.'

Dick was surprised to see that Timmy actually *was* walking! George had cut four big holes in the bottom of the wicker shopping basket – Timmy could put his paws through them and walk along without any difficulty to speak of. He was such a funny sight that Julian and Anne burst out laughing.

'We mustn't let go of the handles,' George warned Dick. 'And if we meet any of the underground staff, I'll tell Timmy to "Sit!" and he'll fold his paws up underneath him. You know what an obedient dog he is.'

It was Dick's turn to laugh. What extraordinary ideas his cousin George did get! They might seem a little mad at times, but they usually turned out quite well in the end.

The Five were soon on the platform, and when George put the basket down and said 'Sit!' Timmy actually did fold his paws up and sat there perfectly still. Some of the other passengers, however, had seen him arriving in his own peculiar means of transport, and there were broad smiles on their faces.

When an underground train drew in, George and Dick heaved the basket containing Timmy into one of the carriages. The four cousins sat on two double seats facing each other, and put the basket down on the floor in between them, close to George's legs.

'What an obedient dog you are, Tim!' said Anne, smiling.

Well, Timmy was certainly obedient. And for a dog, he was above average intelligence. But in spite of all that, he still *was* a dog . . . and dogs have seldom been known to get on very well with cats!

Just at the moment when Anne was praising him, Timmy scented something he didn't like in the carriage. Right at the other end of it, a lady had put a basket with a lid on it down on the floor. A suspicious kind of basket . . . a basket which moved slightly now and then, and gave off a smell of – cat!

'Woof!' barked Timmy at the top of his voice. And forgetting all about George and her orders, he jumped up and dashed forward.

There was a great to-do in the carriage! The passengers were very surprised to see a big walking basket, with four hairy legs and a dog's furious face emerging from it. Some of them were scared, and shrank back in their seats, but most of them were in fits of laughter because Timmy looked so funny.

As for Timmy, he didn't see or hear anyone. It was no use George calling him to heel, or Dick setting off after him. He had reached the basket in no time.

'Woof! Woof!' he barked again, triumphantly. He planted his nose on top of the basket and panted noisily. There was a 'Miaow!' of protest inside, followed by some furious spitting and hissing, and a velvety black paw, with some very sharp claws in it, came shooting out of the air hole on top of the cat basket and hit Timmy on the nose.

'Woof! Ow!' yelped Timmy, retreating. He looked very surprised. Timmy was not a fierce dog, of course, and he knew quite well that he was only pretending to attack the cat. He chased cats for a bit of fun, that was all, and he was simply following the rules of the game as he knew them: it was a dog's business to scare cats! But that stupid cat in its basket didn't seem to understand.

Poor Timmy was baffled. The two handles of his basket were flopping against his sides, which made him look even funnier than he already did, with his disappointed face and his eyes which seemed to be asking for an explanation. There were a couple of drops of blood on his muzzle.

'Well done, Sooty!' said the cat's mistress, amused.

The cat in its basket hissed a little more, but in rather a satisfied sort of way!

George felt too embarrassed by her dog's behaviour to be sorry for him. She grabbed his collar, apologized to the lady with the cat, and took one of the handles of the basket while Dick picked up the

other one. They went back to their seats, carrying
the basket – and to the sound of loud laughter!
George was so upset that she had forgotten to tell
Timmy 'Sit!' – and Timmy, who was upset too,
hadn't thought of folding his legs up. So he was
being carried along in a basket that looked like a
hammock, with his four paws dangling down from
it and almost brushing the floor.

When the Five reached the end of their Tube
journey, George was still pink with embarrassment,
and her cousins were trying their best not to laugh.
As for Timmy, he had no idea what the fuss was
all about.

Once they were up in the fresh air again, George
thankfully let him out of the basket.

'Almond Road must be that big, wide road ahead
of us,' she said.

The children walked up the street till they came
to number 28. It turned out to be a block of large,
old, rather impressive-looking flats. The building
was very well kept, and had just been repainted –
the children thought it was just the sort of place you
might expect a rich old lady to have lived. They rang
the bell at the front door of the building, and an old
woman with a face wrinkled like a withered apple
answered it. She was the caretaker, and she seemed
quite happy to talk to the children. I t was easy to
guess that she liked a good gossip.

'Oh yes, my dear!' she told George. 'I knew Miss
Longfield very well. Poor old lady! She lived on her

own, you know, in a very quiet way, keeping herself to herself. She didn't have many visitors – except from a very old friend of hers, a lady called Mrs Caswell. Yes, I last saw Mrs Caswell on the day of the funeral . . .'

The caretaker sounded as if she would go on talking for hours! George was fidgeting with impatience. Finally she interrupted the old woman's torrent of words.

'Do you know if Mrs Caswell's first name was Elizabeth?'

'Elizabeth, did you say, dear? Yes, I believe it was – now I come to think of it, I'm sure I once heard it.'

'And do you know where she lives?' Dick asked, getting as excited as his cousin.

'Why, yes, it so happens I do. One day Miss Longfield asked me to go and take Mrs Caswell something – it was something she'd got for Mrs Caswell, you see, and so I – '

'Oh, do hurry!' cried George. 'What's her address?'

Her tone took the caretaker aback, and she seemed to close up. Anne, who was always very tactful, gave her nicest smile.

'This is very important for us, you see,' she said. 'We have to find Mrs Caswell to – to tell her of something to her advantage.'

This rather grand sentence was something she had read in a book. The caretaker seemed to be impressed.

'Oh yes, I quite see, dear!' she said. 'Well, Mrs Caswell lives in Heron Street, not far from here.'

The children decided to walk.

The place turned out to be another big block of flats, rather like the one where Miss Longfield used to live. George knocked on the door of the caretaker's flat, and a young woman holding a baby in her arms opened it.

'Hallo,' she said with a smile. 'Can I help you?'

George told her what they had come about. But the young woman shook her head and sighed, sadly.

'I'm so sorry,' she said. 'I'm afraid you're too late. Mrs Caswell died only last week. She caught cold at the funeral of her dear old friend Miss Longfield. And then it turned to pneumonia, and carried her off within forty-eight hours.'

The children looked at each other in dismay. The trail had come to a dead end! Both old ladies were dead – Mrs Caswell, who was to have inherited the pink pearls, and Miss Longfield, who had left them to her. What a sad story!

George was the first to think of something practical. 'I wonder if Mrs Caswell has any family?' she asked. 'A husband, or children?'

'Oh, I think she'd been a widow for a very long time. But I believe she does have a daughter.'

'Do you know where her daughter lives?' asked Julian.

'No, I'm afraid I can't tell you much, because I've only been here two months. But I'm sure there are people living in these flats who'll know more about it than I do. She was a friendly old lady, Mrs Caswell was. She got on well with her neighbours. One of them may be able to help you.'

The children decided to go round knocking at the doors of all the flats in the building. It might take a long time, but it was the only way they could think of to find out what they wanted to know. Unfortunately, most of the people who lived there seemed to be out, but at last, on the same floor as the one with the flat where Mrs Elizabeth Caswell used to live, they found an elderly lady who could give them some help. She asked the children in, and listened carefully to George's explanation.

'Why, yes, Elizabeth did have a daughter,' she said. 'Her name is Denise. She married when she was quite young – that's a long time ago now. I had an invitation to the wedding – with her new address on it, because she and her husband were going to live in a flat her father-in-law was giving them.'

The old lady got out of her chair and went over to a cupboard.

'Well, I never actually went to visit Denise, but I used to see her when she came here to see her mother. And I do believe I kept the address in a notebook somewhere.'

She opened the cupboard and searched inside it for quite a long time. 'Ah, here it is!' she said at last, pleased. 'I've found it. Denise married a man called Lionel Walker. Number 7, Park Avenue, that's where they were living. But goodness knows if they're still there. It's all so long ago . . . and it's ages since Denise has been here. I'm afraid she had some kind of a quarrel with her mother – very unfortunate, but these things do happen in a family.'

George quickly copied down Denise Walker's address, thanked the old lady, and said goodbye. She hurried down the stairs, with her cousins and Timmy after her.

'Right!' she said, when they were out in the road again. 'Since Mrs Caswell's dead, it's her daughter who will inherit the pink pearls. Now, where's Park Avenue, Julian?'

Julian, resourceful as usual, had thought of bringing the street map of the city with him. He took it out of his pocket and looked at it. 'Bother!' he said. 'It's near the Botanic Gardens! We'll have to take a bus to get there!'

When he said 'bus' George and Timmy both looked at the big basket Dick was carrying, at the same time.

'Oh, come on!' said Dick, laughing. 'We'll manage! Here, Timmy, jump in, and no putting your paws through the bottom of the basket this time. After all, we shan't have to change – just heave you once into the bus and once out again, and that won't kill us!'

Twenty minutes later, the children got out of the bus in front of the block of flats where the Walkers lived. Or where they *once* lived! Were the Five about to lose the scent after they had come so far?

Still on the Trail

Timmy, delighted to get a chance to stretch his legs at last, went leaping all round George.

'Stop it, Timmy!' she told her dog. 'Don't act up like that! We're on a very serious mission.'

So Timmy calmed down, like the good dog he was. The Five wanted to find the caretaker to ask for information. They saw a man sweeping the entrance hall. He stood in their way.

'What are you kids after?' he asked in a surly tone.

'We want to ask the caretaker for some information,' said Julian politely.

'I'm the caretaker. Go ahead, then!' said the man, still sounding very unfriendly.

'Well, I wonder if you could tell us whether Mrs Denise Walker still lives here?' asked Julian.

'Mrs Walker? Oh, I'm afraid the Walkers died in a crash years ago, though it wasn't surprising either. That son-in-law of theirs used to drive like a maniac! Young folk have no common sense at all, these days. Now if *I* could afford a car . . .'

George, Julian, Dick and Anne kept quiet. It was all getting rather sad. Whenever they thought they'd found out what they wanted, they turned out to have come up against a blank wall because the person who ought to have inherited those magnificent pink pearls was dead.

However, George had made a mental note of the fact that the Walkers had a son-in-law. If you have a son-in-law, you need to have a daughter first. Therefore, the Walkers had had a daughter, George proudly deduced. But had the daughter been in the crash with them? Did *she* die with her parents or was she still alive? There were still an awful lot of question marks.

In the end George felt too impatient to go on listening to the caretaker's grievances, and she interrupted as politely as she could.

'Did Mr and Mrs Walker's daughter live with them?' she asked. 'If she didn't, can you give us her address? Oh, and her married name too.'

'And would there be anything else, young fellow?' asked the caretaker sarcastically, thinking George was a boy, as so many people did when they first met her. He wasn't pleased by the interruption, either. 'Do you kids think I'm an information bureau or what? Go on, clear out! Out, I said! Can't you see that nasty dog of yours is making dirty marks all over my clean floor?'

George was about to leap to Timmy's defence, as usual, but Julian tactfully intervened. 'Since you can't tell us what we want to know,' he said coolly, 'I think we'll ask the Walkers' neighbours. They may be able to tell us something.'

'You're not going up those stairs, not if I know it!' the caretaker exploded. 'I've just swept those stairs, I have!'

'We'll carry Timmy!' Dick promised.

'And we'll wipe our feet *very* well before we go up!' Anne assured the caretaker, with her sweetest smile. But even that didn't melt his heart.

'Nothing doing!' he shouted. 'You just get out, and take that nasty brute with you. I can't stand here wasting time talking to the likes of you!'

'There are some caretakers I wouldn't want taking care of anything of *mine*!' muttered George darkly, under her breath.

But the unpleasant caretaker caught what she said. He was furious, and raised his broom as if he were about to chase the children away with it. However, he'd reckoned without Timmy! The faithful dog thought the caretaker meant to harm his beloved George, and he leaped forward, baring his teeth, and barking furiously.

Surprised as much as frightened, the caretaker dropped his broom. George just had time to grab her dog's collar.

'You've got no right to stop us knocking on people's doors!' she told the caretaker. 'And still less right to threaten us! We're doing no harm, just trying to get some information about people we want to find.'

The caretaker's face, which was already rather red, was practically purple with rage now!

'I . . . I . . . you . . . you . . .' he stammered, sounding frightened and angry at the same time.

'Look here, if you go on like that my cousin might set her dog on you, you know!' Dick pointed out to the man.

Even Julian was not so calm as usual, for once. The caretaker's aggressive attitude wasn't called for at all, and really annoyed him. 'And if she does, we can all say we saw you attack him!' he said.

The caretaker obviously thought it would be more sensible to beat a retreat to his own flat – which he did, slamming the door behind him.

George started laughing. 'Well, he's safe from Timmy's teeth in there!' she said. 'Well done, Tim! Good work! Thanks to you, we can go on with our inquiries.'

'Come on, then,' said Dick. 'Let's go up.'

They all made for the staircase. When they got to the first floor, Julian rang the first doorbell on the right. A young woman opened the door.

'Good afternoon,' said Julian, smiling politely. 'We're very sorry to bother you, but we're looking for the daughter of Mr and Mrs Walker who used to live here. Do you by any chance know her address?'

'Walker?' asked the woman. 'I'm afraid I don't know anyone called Walker in this block of flats, though of course I only moved here a little while ago. I wish I could help, but . . . oh, wait a minute, I have an idea! Go on up to the fourth floor! There's an old gentleman who had a flat up there, called Mr Somerville – he's a music teacher, and he's been living in this building for over thirty years. I'm sure he'll be able to tell you what you want to know.'

'Thank you very much,' said the children, and they hurried up to the fourth floor. Sure enough, the first door on the left had a brass plate on it saying 'Mark Somerville – Piano Teacher'.

George rang the bell at once, and the door was opened almost immediately by a tall old man with a slight stoop. The children took to Mr Somerville at first sight – he had such a kind face, and a very friendly smile. His thick white hair was like a kind of halo round his head.

'Well, good afternoon, young people!' he said. 'What can I do for you? Have you come to ask about piano lessons?'

George smiled back at Mr Somerville. 'No, it isn't that,' she said. 'Could we talk to you in private for a moment?'

'Of course, my boy,' agreed Mr Somerville. Like the caretaker, *he* thought George was a boy! 'Come along in, all four of you – I beg your pardon, I should say all *five* of you!' he added, spotting Timmy, who was obeying a command from George and carefully wiping his paws on the mat. 'What a nice dog! Yours, is he, young man?'

George didn't mind being taken for a boy a bit – she smiled at Mr Somerville again. 'Actually, I'm afraid I'm *not* a boy!' she explained, rather regretfully. 'But yes, Timmy *is* my dog, and he's intelligent as well as nice, aren't you, Timmy? In fact, at the moment he's helping us in some detective inquiries!' she added.

Timmy gave Mr Somerville a paw, and Mr Somerville solemnly shook it. 'A real sleuth hound, I see!' he said.

So then Julian explained what they had come about. The music teacher was not smiling so broadly when he had finished.

'I see,' said Mr Somerville. 'Yes, what the caretaker told you was right, and it's a sad story. They were very pleasant people. But, I'm glad to say Angela is still alive. She wasn't with her parents and her husband at the time of the accident. I've known Angela since she was a baby – I used to give her piano lessons when she was small. She was really very good at music, one of my best pupils. In fact now that she's grown up – she was twenty-seven this year – she teaches the piano herself. She has to earn a living for herself and her little girl Monica, you see.'

'What's her married name?' asked George.

'And where does she live?' added Dick.

'Angela's married name is Mrs Trevor. She has a little two-roomed flat not so very far from here – it's in Sycamore Road,' Mr Somerville told the children.

The Five looked at each other triumphantly. At last they were really getting somewhere!

'Thank you very much, sir!' said Julian gratefully. 'You see, we're anxious to find Angela Trevor to tell her she's inherited something very valuable!'

Mr Somerville was too polite to ask a lot of questions. He simply said, 'Well, I'm delighted to hear it! Angela is such a good, hard-working person, and she really deserves a bit of luck after all the trouble she's had.'

'Where exactly *is* Sycamore Road?' Dick asked. Just then a young man of about eighteen came bursting in through the door. Timmy barked at him.

'Now, now, don't eat Thomas up!' Mr Somerville told the dog, laughing. 'Thomas is my grandson – he won't hurt you!'

When the children had been introduced, Thomas offered to show them the way to Sycamore Road. 'It's not far from here, but you might miss the turn into the road – the street name isn't very obvious. It'll save you time if I just go with you,' he said.

The children were happy to accept his offer. They said goodbye to Mr Somerville and followed Thomas, who seemed very nice – and very talkative too.

'I say, I think I've heard of you before!' he told

the children. 'Aren't you the children they call the Five – you and your dog, I mean? Yes, I thought so! You've been in the papers several times. Didn't you outwit the criminal called the Black Mask, and discover the treasure in the Golden Galleon?'

'That's right!' said Dick, smiling. 'What a memory you've got!'

'Well, *you've* got quite a reputation, you know! Listen – if you need any more help while you're staying in this town, I'd be happy to lend a hand. My father lets me borrow his car sometimes. That might be useful. Look, here's my telephone number.'

Julian carefully put the piece of paper Thomas handed him away in his wallet. Then they arrived outside the flats in Sycamore Road where Angela Trevor lived. The children thanked their new friend, said goodbye, and Thomas went off again to visit his grandfather, as he had planned to do.

The flats in Sycamore Road didn't look as grand as the blocks where old Miss Longfield and Mrs Caswell used to live, and there wasn't any caretaker. However, there were names on a plate by the front door, and the children saw that 'A. Trevor' lived on the second floor. They climbed the stairs, and Julian rang the doorbell.

There was no answer. Julian waited a few seconds, and then tried again. Still no luck! No doubt about it – Angela Trevor must be out.

'Too bad!' sighed Dick. 'We'll just have to come back tomorrow!'

All the same, the children agreed, it had been an interesting and successful afternoon. They were feeling quite pleased with themselves when they got back to Cousin Jane's flat and told Aunt Fanny about the results of their inquiries. She was delighted to hear that it looked as if they really had tracked down Mrs Caswell's granddaughter, who would now be the right person to inherit the pink pearls.

The children went to bed quite early that night – all that walking about in the wintry air had made them more tired than they were going to admit to Aunt Fanny and Uncle Quentin. George went to sleep feeling very happy. She could just imagine how delighted Angela Trevor would be when she heard their news about the wonderful necklace of pink pearls.

In the middle of the night, George had a dream. She dreamed that the pink pearls were lying displayed on the faded velvet upholstery of the tub chair. All of a sudden a man appeared – it was Ernest Parry, whom the children had christened Frog-face. He grinned and put out a hand for the pink pearls. George opened her mouth to shout, but only a low growl came out . . .

She woke up with a start. The low growl was real, and not a dream, but it didn't come from her – it was Timmy growling! He was on the alert by the door of the bedroom George and Anne were sharing, his nose close to the ground. He must have heard something. George jumped out of bed.

'Ssh!' she told him in a low voice, putting her slippers on. 'Let me listen, Timmy.'

She put her ear close to the door, trying to catch the sound which had roused Timmy. And sure enough, there was a faint, very faint creaking noise, coming from the sitting-room.

— 5 —

A Burglar in the Night

Very quietly, George tiptoed over to her cousin and shook Anne by the shoulder. 'Anne!' she whispered. 'Wake up! Timmy's on the alert. I'm sure there's a burglar in the flat. Follow me, and don't make any noise. We must find out what's up!'

'We'd better tell Uncle Quentin and the boys,' Anne whispered back.

'No, that would be bound to alarm the burglar and give him time to get away. Come on, quick, get up!'

Anne obeyed without any more protests. George had already opened the bedroom door. She made her way out into the passage with Anne after her. The sitting-room was directly opposite their bedroom. The door was just ajar, and a faint glimmer of light showed through it. Seeing that, Timmy couldn't restrain himself any longer. He rushed at the door, barking furiously, and pushed it open. Without thinking of the danger, George ran into the room after him.

'Uncle Quentin!' shouted Anne. 'Julian! Dick! Come here, quickly!'

There was a great to-do all over the flat. George had dashed into the sitting-room at such speed, she almost collided with a man who was standing beside the tub chair Aunt Fanny had bought at the auction sale. The faint light came from a torch which he had put down on the floor. George could make out nothing but the man's vague shape – however, she saw that he was quickly withdrawing his hand from the space down the back of the chair.

'Timmy – get him!' she ordered.

The burglar let out a furious exclamation, and made for the French windows, which were standing wide open. Timmy was after him at once – he didn't need any more orders from his mistress to know what she wanted him to do. He got his teeth into one of the man's trouser-legs, but the man pulled himself free and reached the balcony.

The children decided afterwards that he must have got away by jumping from there to the balcony of the flat next door, and then running down the fire escape. Anyway, when Aunt Fanny, Uncle Quentin and the boys arrived on the scene, they found no one but George and Timmy in the sitting-room.

'It was a burglar all right,' said George. 'I didn't see him very clearly, but I'm sure it was that frog-faced man, Ernest Parry! He was leaning over the chair, and he seemed to be looking for something down the back of the seat.'

'The pink pearls!' said Dick.

'Yes, of course, and that just shows that what I thought before is right!' said George. 'That man *knew* the necklace was hidden somewhere in that chair, even before it went to the auction sale.'

'And that's why he was so keen to buy it back from Aunt Fanny,' agreed Anne.

'Now, children, you mustn't go accusing people without any proof!' Uncle Quentin interrupted, rather sternly. 'After all, we don't know anything positive.'

'But our theories do hold water, Uncle Quentin,' Julian pointed out in his sensible way.

'I'm not saying they don't, Julian. But they won't be enough for the police. They'll need some kind of solid evidence. And since nothing seems to be missing from this room, we've only been the victims of an *attempted* burglary. I shall certainly report it to the police tomorrow, but I can't accuse Ernest Parry of being the burglar – after all, you only saw a man's shape, George. We must go cautiously.'

Aunt Fanny had taken a quick look round the room, and she confirmed that nothing had actually been stolen. Julian and Dick found some marks on the French windows to the balcony, where the burglar had obviously forced it open to let himself in. Uncle Quentin knew there was not much the police could do with so little to go on in the way of clues.

George, Dick and Anne went back to bed still convinced that the burglar had been Ernest Parry. Julian was the only one to agree with his uncle so far as to say that there *might* be some doubt in it – but that was just Julian being fair-minded as usual! George knew he really thought the same as they did.

'Well, if the police can't do anything about him without evidence,' muttered George rather crossly, getting between the sheets again, 'there's nothing to stop *us* taking a hand! Is there, Timmy, old boy?'

'Woof!' said Timmy decidedly, from the bedside rug where he had settled down again.

'Anyway,' said Anne, 'it's a good thing those pearls weren't still in the tub chair. Whoever the burglar may be, he couldn't know that Aunt Fanny's keeping them safe in her handbag until we can give them to Angela Trevor.'

A grunt was the only reply. After all that excitement, George had fallen asleep! Timmy was asleep as well, and it wasn't long before Anne dropped off herself.

Next morning, when Uncle Quentin had gone off to his conference, saying he would report the attempted burglary to the police on the way, the Five sat at the breakfast table for quite a long time, discussing last night's events. Aunt Fanny had finished her own breakfast, and was busy in the kitchen.

'I'm absolutely positive the burglar was Ernest Parry!' George said again.

'I'm not quite so sure of that now,' said Julian, frowning. 'One thing that occurred to me in the night is that Parry's shop, selling curios and souvenirs, must be quite a profitable business – Mimosa Avenue is obviously a good area of town. If Parry knew about the pearls, which I do agree seems likely, I believe he might have gone as far as trying to buy the chair back, but not any further. I honestly can't see him breaking into the flat and doing athletic leaps from balcony to balcony!'

'But who else could have known both that the pearls were hidden in the tub chair *and* that Aunt Fanny had bought it?' asked Dick.

'I didn't like Mr Parry at all,' said Anne. 'I agree with George. He must have been last night's burglar!'

'It *was* him!' said George.

'But how can you prove it?' sighed Julian.

George grinned. 'Well, I think we *may* have a real clue, whatever my father thought last night! Look at this!'

She took a scrap of navy-blue fabric out of her pocket and waved it under her cousins' noses.

'Look! A bit of material Timmy tore away from our burglar's trousers – which means we have proof of what he was wearing last night! Isn't it wonderful? This scrap of fabric will have its owner's scent on it – and thanks to his excellent nose, Timmy will be able to identify that owner. I'm going to take him to Parry's shop, and if Timmy reacts to the sight of the shopkeeper – '

'We still won't have anything but one more reason to suspect him,' Julian finished her sentence for her. 'Timmy's reactions wouldn't be *proof*, you know.'

'Well, at least it'll make us certain enough to concentrate on Ernest Parry,' George pointed out. 'He does want those pearls, and I don't think he's giving up so easily!'

'But if we go to Mr Parry's shop he'll realize we suspect him,' Anne pointed out. 'And then he'll be so suspicious of *us*, it'll be difficult for us to keep watch on him or anything like that.'

'It'll be all right!' said George cheerfully. 'He doesn't actually know us, does he? He can hardly have noticed us in all the crowd at the sale – he was too busy concentrating on my mother, because she was outbidding him for the chair.'

'Yes, George is right,' Dick agreed. 'And when he came here trying to buy it from her, we were in the next room.'

'He saw you last night, though, George,' said Julian. 'In the sitting-room.'

'I shouldn't think he can have seen any more than a vague shape – that was all I saw of *him*,' George said.

'What about Timmy, though?' asked Anne, smiling. 'He didn't just *see* Timmy – he felt him too! He only just got away.'

'Woof!' agreed Timmy, sounding pleased with himself.

George thought about Anne's objection, weighing up the pros and cons of it. Then she looked up with a defiant light in her eyes. 'Well, never mind that!' she said. 'We'll take a chance – I do so want to find out for certain about Mr Parry. But we won't play all our cards at once. I'll go into the shop first, with Timmy. He doesn't know the rest of you at all – so if my suspicions turn out to be right, you can easily go in after me!'

Julian had several objections to this idea, but George stuck to her guns. An hour later, after showing Timmy the scrap of material and making him have a good sniff at it, she set off with the dog. Her cousins were following, keeping a good distance behind her. They stopped several doors away from Mr Parry's curio and souvenir shop in Mimosa Avenue, to wait for George there.

George gave Timmy one last sniff at the fabric from the burglar's trousers, and then marched boldly into the shop.

Ernest Parry was there by himself. When he saw George, he came forward with an oily smile. 'What can I do for you?' he asked.

But George had no time to reply – Timmy had recognized last night's visitor, and was getting ready to jump at his throat! George only just managed to stop him.

'Oh, I'm so sorry!' she said calmly. 'I really don't

know what's come over him – he's such a good dog usually.'

A look of panic had come into Parry's eyes – and was quickly replaced by a look of suspicion. George was quite sure of it now! Timmy had just identified their burglar. On the other hand, the burglar had also recognized the dog that attacked him last night.

'Go away, and take your dog with you!' snapped Parry. 'I don't allow animals in this shop.'

George meekly retreated. She was beginning to regret her idea of coming to the shop – Parry was going to be on his guard against her now.

She walked slowly back to her cousins. Julian, as might have been expected, was not pleased to hear that possibly she – and certainly Timmy – had been recognized. Deep in discussion, the children didn't notice Parry who, almost the moment George left it, had come out of his shop, locked the door and put a 'Closed' notice on it, and then followed her. The wind was blowing the wrong way for Timmy to catch his scent. He was now hiding behind a parked car – and listening to every word the children said!

'All right, Ju, I admit I may have been wrong to walk into the enemy camp like that,' said George ruefully, 'but at least I'm absolutely certain now that that man is determined to get hold of the pink pearls. We must get Angela Trevor's legacy to her as soon as we possibly can!'

'Well, why don't we go and see her now?' suggested Dick. 'She was out yesterday evening, but she may be in today.'

'Oh yes, let's!' cried Anne, delighted at the idea. 'She'll be so pleased to hear about her good luck.'

So off the children went, back to Sycamore Road. As they went in at the front door of the block of flats where Angela Trevor lived, George happened to glance behind her.

'My word!' she exclaimed. 'I do believe I saw Parry just slipping into cover round the corner there!'

'You're obsessed with Parry, that's what it is, George!' said Dick, laughing. 'Seeing him everywhere! Come on, here we are.'

The children were in luck today – Angela Trevor herself came to the door as soon as they rang the bell. She looked very young to be a widow. She had long dark hair flowing over her shoulders. Her little girl Monica was with her – she was fair-haired, with a snub nose and a lovely smile, and looked as if she was about six.

Julian introduced himself and the others, and asked if they could have a private word with her. Angela Trevor smiled at the serious look on the children's faces.

'Is it something important?' she asked.

'Yes, very important!'

'Come in and sit down, then,' said Angela. 'I'm listening!'

Speaking in turn, the children told her all about their extraordinary adventure. After a while Monica stopped playing with Timmy and listened too.

'Why, that's amazing!' said Angela, when the children had finished their tale. 'I can hardly believe it!'

'It's true, though!' George assured her. 'Look, if you want to make sure, why not ring my mother?' she added, pointing to a telephone in the corner of the room. 'She'll tell you all about it!'

And after a phone conversation with Aunt Fanny, Angela had no more doubts that her legacy was real. She was delighted! Hugging Monica happily, she thanked the Five warmly.

'Thanks to you and Granny's old friend, dear Miss Longfield, I shall be able to live without pinching and scraping all the time, and give Monica a few more treats! I've just been able to earn a living for both of us with my music teaching over the last few years, but it's been hard work – this good luck is just wonderful! What a Christmas we shall have now!'

'I'm sure the necklace must be very, very valuable,' Julian said. 'Pink pearls are extremely rare.'

'And so pretty, too,' said Anne, who loved beautiful things.

'Your mother has just given me some very good advice over the telephone,' said Angela, turning to George. 'She thought I ought to get the necklace valued as soon as possible, and then sell it and invest the money from its sale. I've decided to do exactly as she suggests.'

'Good!' said George. 'And now all you have to do is come back with us and pick up your pearls!'

Angela smiled a little apologetically. 'There's nothing I'd like to do better!' she said. 'But I'm afraid I shall have to stay here all day. I have a full timetable of lessons, and I can't let my pupils down just because I've had such an amazing windfall. Perhaps I could come tomorrow, if that suits your mother, George? I should very much like to meet her – and I was so surprised and excited that I forgot to thank her properly over the phone just now!'

George rang her mother back again at once, and Aunt Fanny said that of course Angela could come and see her next day. She wouldn't be going out all morning, she said, so any time after about ten o'clock would suit her perfectly.

Angela was delighted. 'See you tomorrow, then!' she told the children as they said goodbye. 'And many, many thanks for all you've done for me and Monica!'

'See you tomorrow!' repeated Monica, who didn't seem to want to part from Anne and Timmy. Anne loved small children, and thought Monica was adorable. She was hoping that Angela would bring her daughter with her the next day.

And so she did! After the children had been out to do Aunt Fanny's shopping for the day, they kept watch from the French windows looking out on to the balcony over the street, to see when Angela arrived. 'There they are!' said Dick all of a sudden. 'Both of them. They must have walked, unless they came on the bus which stops just round the corner!'

'Oh, I'm so glad Monica's with her mother!' said Anne.

'I'll go and tell Aunt Fanny they're here,' said Julian.

Dick and Anne went away from the window too, but George stayed at her post. Something, or rather someone, had attracted her attention.

A man had just come round the corner of the road – and it looked very much as if he were following Angela, taking great care she didn't notice him.

'I may be wrong,' muttered George to herself, 'but something about that shape reminds me of someone – such as Mr Ernest Parry! What do *you* think, Timmy?'

'Grr!' said Timmy, with his nose pressed to the window. 'Woof!'

'Of course,' George went on, talking to herself as much as her dog, 'I can't be sure of it. Seen from up here, he looks more like a scarecrow, wearing a long overcoat with the collar turned up and a hat pulled right down over his eyes. If it really is Parry, he's doing his best to disguise himself.'

'Woof!' Timmy agreed again.

George decided she'd better go and find her cousins. 'Listen!' she told them breathlessly. 'Something's up! It looks to me as if somehow, though

goodness knows just *how*, Ernest Parry knows
exactly what's been going on – and the proof
of it is that he's followed Angela and Monica
here!'

— 6 —

The Pearls in Peril

'You must be dreaming!' said Dick. 'How could he possibly know that . . .'

'Ssh!' Anne interrupted. 'There goes the door-bell!'

Of course it was Angela and her daughter. Aunt Fanny welcomed them in, telling them how glad she was to see them. Then she went to find the blue box, which was safe in her bag in the bedroom, and gave it to Angela. Fingers shaking, Angela lifted the lid and stared at the beautiful double row of pink pearls.

'What an unexpected, marvellous Christmas present!' she cried. 'These pearls are beautiful – the necklace must be worth a fortune.'

'I'm sure it is!' Aunt Fanny agreed. 'And I can tell you,' she added, laughing, 'I'm very glad to be able to get rid of it and hand it over to its rightful owner. I wouldn't have liked the responsibility of looking after something so precious much longer.'

'No, because do you know, somebody tried to

burgle us!' Dick told Angela. 'A man broke in here the night before last. Luckily George and Timmy chased him off again!'

'What?' cried Angela, with a nervous start. 'Oh dear – I'm so sorry. Do you think he was really after these pearls, then?'

'We're sure he was,' said Dick, and he told the whole story, including – although Aunt Fanny looked rather annoyed about this – George's suspicions of Ernest Parry. By now, all her cousins shared those suspicions too.

'Really, Dick, you can't go accusing people without any proof!' Aunt Fanny told her nephew, sounding cross. 'George does sometimes jump to conclusions, you know.'

George herself, who had been rather quiet and thoughtful up to this point, interrupted Aunt Fanny. 'Honestly, Mother, it's quite true, and in fact I'm still rather worried. When I was looking out of the window just now I thought I saw a man following Mrs Trevor – a man who looked very like Parry in disguise!'

'As I said before, you must be dreaming, George!' Dick repeated. 'How on earth could he have known about Angela?'

'I've no idea how,' said George, gloomily, 'but there we are, he did. Monica and her mother have been followed to this flat.'

Angela had gone white as a sheet. 'So I wasn't imagining things!' she breathed.

'Imagining things? Imagining what?' asked George.

'I – well, I did think there was a man in a long overcoat keeping a little way behind us when we went out. And then he boarded the same bus as we did . . . I couldn't make his face out very well.'

At once, Julian and Dick ran to the French windows, opened them and leaned out over the balcony. But they couldn't see any suspicious-looking man anywhere.

'Nothing to report!' said Julian, coming back into the sitting-room. 'Either the man who was following you had gone away, or he only *seemed* to be following you and was there by chance.'

'I don't think that was it,' said George. 'I'm sure he *meant* to follow Angela. I saw him myself, Ju. He was trying to pass unnoticed, but I could tell it was Parry.'

'If he's still hanging about, Angela,' said Dick, 'he must be hiding somewhere, ready to go on following you – he may try to steal your pearls!'

'Don't dramatize things so, Dick!' said Aunt Fanny.

'Listen!' George said, turning to Angela. 'I think the most urgent thing now is to deposit that necklace in a bank vault!'

'That's a very good idea!' Angela agreed. 'And my bank is quite close to where I live.'

'Then you better go straight there. And I don't think it would be very sensible for you to go on your own, in the circumstances, so why don't my cousins and I come with you? If he sees you with so many other people, Parry won't dare to do anything.'

Angela Trevor seemed cheered by this offer. 'How kind of you, George!' she said. 'I'll be happy to have your company – that is, if your mother agrees?' she added, turning rather timidly to Aunt Fanny.

'Yes, of course,' said Aunt Fanny. 'But I really don't think you're in the slightest danger, you know!' And she went on, smiling, 'You'd better go by Tube – there's an Underground station not far away. However, I'm sure that George is wrong and no one has any designs on your pearls. My daughter has a very lively imagination.'

Angela put the precious box into her bag, and then, after saying goodbye to Aunt Fanny, she and Monica left with the Five. Once they were out in the street, the children looked around them, but in vain. There was no sign of their suspect.

They very soon reached the way into the Underground station, and went down the steps to the platform. Timmy had resigned himself to travelling in a basket. After his adventures the last time he went on the Tube, George wasn't letting him use the one with holes for his legs in any more!

They waited in silence for the train to come in. Angela Trevor was anxious to get to her bank as soon as possible. The children, who were standing a little way behind her, were taking their job as bodyguards very seriously. Anne was holding Monica's hand,

and George and Dick were holding the basket with Timmy in it – poor dog, he *did* feel silly.

Then the train arrived. Angela, who was clutching her bag with the precious necklace in it, happened to be standing very near the edge of the platform – and all of a sudden, a man came up beside her and snatched the bag, jostling her quite violently. Angela swayed, lost her balance – and would have fallen under the train if George and Dick hadn't grabbed hold of her at once.

Taking advantage of the hurry and bustle on the platform, the man made off through the crowd of passengers, going towards the exit barrier. Most of the people in the station had seen nothing of the incident – and they all wanted to board the train, anyway. The thief would have got away but for Julian and Timmy. They gave chase! Timmy, leaping out of his basket, soon caught up with the man.

Their thief, who looked like a disreputable old tramp, let out a cry of fear when the dog jumped on him. Next moment, Julian had caught up too. He snatched Angela Trevor's bag back from the thief again.

Panic-stricken, the man kept his raised right arm in front of his face, as if to shield it, while Timmy stopped him getting away by hanging on to his other arm. Julian was going to grab him too when a station official came up. Seizing Timmy by the collar, he dragged him off the thief, shouting, 'Let go, will you, you brute? Attacking people because they don't happen to be well dressed! What's more, dogs aren't allowed loose on the platforms. Is he yours, young man?' asked the official, turning to Julian. 'Well, just you wait! You could find yourself in trouble! Letting a dog loose like this!'

It was no good Julian trying to explain – the station official simply wouldn't listen. He pulled at the dog's collar so hard that poor Timmy was half strangled. And of course, the 'tramp' took advantage of the argument to get away.

He was gone in a twinkling, disappearing so fast that Julian couldn't even see where he went. Anyway, the station official wouldn't let him set off in pursuit.

'Look here, boy, did you hear what I was saying?' he asked angrily. But at this moment George, Dick and Anne came to the rescue, followed by Angela, who was still shaking from her fright, and Monica, who had burst into tears.

'You leave my dog alone!' George ordered the man. She was furious to see someone ill-treating her beloved Timmy. 'Can't you see he was stopping a thief!'

'Yes, he really was – that man who's just got away stole my bag and tried to push me under the train!' Angela assured the official. 'Oh, George! You and Dick saved my life – and Julian and dear Timmy got my pearls back!'

She burst into tears. The station official, who

hadn't been willing to listen to Julian, believed Angela, and looked very crestfallen. 'Dear me – I'm so sorry, madam,' he stammered. 'How was I to know?'

Julian was in a hurry. 'Let's get moving!' he suggested. 'My mind won't be at ease until we're safely at the bank.'

Timmy climbed back into his basket, and they all got into a carriage of the next train to come in. Nobody said a word until they were in daylight again. Up in the street, they looked around them, fearing the worst. But there was no suspicious figure lurking near by.

'Quick!' said Angela. 'My bank is in the next street.'

'Yes,' said George, 'you must hurry to get those pearls into safety. And then we'll see about Parry!'

'Parry,' gasped Angela. 'You don't really think the man in the Tube station was Parry, do you?'

'Of course I do!' said George. 'He may have tried disguising himself as a tramp, but *I* recognized him – at the moment he attacked you!'

'Then you think he must have been following us ever since we left home?' said Dick.

'Yes, I do,' said George. 'He must have been keeping watch on us from the cover of the news-stand in the street. He wouldn't have had to do much to change his appearance: make a dent or so in his hat, wipe a bit of dirt over his face and hands, sweep the ground with his overcoat to make it look shabby.

If he did that, Angela, he could feel pretty sure that even if you had noticed he was following you on your way to us, you wouldn't recognize him again – or not straight away, in any case.'

'But for that stupid man at the station, we'd have him by now! We caught him red-handed!'

'Or dirty-handed, anyway,' said Anne, and this rather feeble joke made everyone relax. Next moment, Angela heaved a sigh of relief.

'Here we are!' she said. 'This is my bank! I'll go and rent a safe and put the pearls inside it. Would you look after Monica for me while I go and see the manager? I'll meet you here in the lobby.'

And a little later, the necklace was safely locked away. Parry hadn't a hope of getting his hands on it now – whether they were red *or* dirty!

'All's well that ends well,' said Julian, with satisfaction. 'I think we've done all right! We found the pearls, and the will, and we delivered the legacy to Angela its rightful owner. Well done the Five!'

Julian thought that was the end of the story – but next day, an unexpected telephone call from Angela stirred everything up again. Aunt Fanny had gone out when Angela rang, so it was George who answered the phone.

'Hallo?' said Angela, at the other end of the line. 'Oh, George dear, is that you? Oh, this is dreadful – dreadful . . .'

'What is? What's happened?' asked George at once.

'This morning – there was an anonymous letter, slipped under my door! It was threatening me – a kind of blackmail – oh, George, I just don't know what to do!'

A little shiver ran down George's spine. She couldn't quite have said whether it was a shiver of alarm or of anticipation at the prospect of another adventure. But poor Angela sounded terribly upset. 'Calm down,' George advised her. 'Now, tell me all about it. Exactly what threats did this letter make?'

'It said – it said my little Monica would be kidnapped if I didn't hand over the pearl necklace!'

'*What*?' said George. 'What did you say?' She could hardly grasp it!

Angela explained, speaking very fast. 'The letter – it was full of detailed instructions. I'm to hand over the pearls as soon as I've been to the bank to fetch them. Oh, George, it does me so much good to tell you all about it! I've made up my mind to do what these people want, and never mind the money! Monica's safety matters more.'

'Hang on – wait a minute!' George shouted down the phone. 'Angela, don't ring off yet! Give me a moment to think – and tell the others.'

It didn't take long to do that. Julian, Dick and Anne were horrified and indignant.

'What a terrible, cowardly thing to do!' said Julian. 'An anonymous blackmailer – '

'Not exactly anonymous!' George reminded her cousin. 'It must be Ernest Parry again. Julian, you pick up the extension and listen in.' She spoke into the receiver again. 'Angela, are you still there? Look, we think you ought to phone the police. They'll send someone to look after you.'

'Oh, George – the anonymous letter told me not to go to the police – and I couldn't expect a police bodyguard for my little girl indefinitely. Once they'd left, Monica would be in just as much danger as before,' said Angela tearfully.

Julian was thinking hard. Aunt Fanny and Uncle Quentin were both out, or the children could have turned to them for advice. But in any case, he thought this was something much too serious for the Five to tackle on their own. Taking the receiver from George, he tried to persuade Angela to ignore the instructions in the letter.

'George is right, Angela,' he said. 'You must go to the police. Honestly, it's the only sensible thing to do.'

'But I daren't disobey the letter, Julian! I'm so scared of what might happen. I shouldn't even have telephoned *you* – I wasn't to tell anyone. But I was at my wits' end. I needed to talk to somebody. Anyway,' said Angela firmly, 'I've made up my mind. I'm going to the bank, and then I'm going to the meeting place alone. I'll give up the pearls, and then I'll be left in peace. Monica's safety comes first – I know you'll understand.'

Realizing he would never persuade her, Julian tried threats instead. 'Look, if *you* don't go to the police, we'll do it for you,' he said. 'We're going to protect you whatever you do.'

Angela laughed sadly. 'I don't think you can! The police won't listen to you. The only evidence of Monica's danger is the anonymous letter, and I've got that. The police wouldn't believe your story with nothing to back it up. Thank you all so much for wanting to help me – it's so kind of you, but I'm afraid there's nothing you can do. However, thank you all the same, children!'

George, who was listening in on the extension, realized that Angela was about to hang up, and she quickly took the receiver from Julian. 'Angela, don't ring off yet!' she begged. 'Tell us exactly what the detailed instructions in the letter said. What have you got to do once you've taken the pearls out of the bank? Where are you supposed to be meeting this horrible person?'

'George, I'm not telling you anything else. I've talked too much already,' said Angela, and she added, sighing, 'I'll hope to see you later, when this wretched business is all over. And thank you again for your sympathy, George dear. Goodbye!'

A click on the line told George that Angela really had hung up this time. The boys looked quite horrified and Anne was nearly crying. George herself, though seldom at a loss for an idea, was baffled for the moment, but she was also thinking hard.

'Cheer up, everyone!' she said firmly, in a minute or so. 'We're not going to just let this happen. We must *do* something – and I've just thought what! Here's my plan. We'll keep watch on the entrance to the bank, wait for Angela to come out, and follow her to this meeting place she won't tell us about. And then we'll take action!'

'Exactly how?' asked Dick, who didn't think much of his cousin's idea. 'For a start, Angela will be going to her bank at once, and it's only in the next street to hers. We'd never get there in time!'

'Maybe we could,' said George. 'Quick, Ju – give me that phone number, will you? The one Thomas Somerville gave you. Now or never is the time to call on him for help!'

7

Thomas Lends a Hand

A moment or so later, George had Thomas on the line. Her cousins were crowding around the telephone, listening in to the conversation.

'Hallo, Thomas! It's George Kirrin – the Five, you remember meeting us at your grandfather's? Listen, if possible we need your help. Can you really borrow your father's car – and could you be here very quickly? In ten minutes . . . yes, that's marvellous! It's something very, very urgent, and every minute counts. Thanks very much indeed, Thomas! We'll be down on the pavement outside these flats, waiting for you!'

George put the phone down, and turned to the others.

'He's coming!' she said. 'We may win the race against time after all! Angela will have to find someone to look after Monica before she goes out – maybe she'll take her to a neighbour. And then she'll be going to the bank. But she'll have to go down to the bank vault, and sign things, and go to her safe, open it and take the pearls out. I hope we'll be there before she leaves the bank.'

The Five raced downstairs, and they didn't have long to wait before Thomas drove up in his father's car. The young man gave them a cheery wave. 'In you jump!' he said. 'This car isn't large, but I think we'll all fit in. Now, where do you want to go?'

Julian told him, and Thomas set off as fast as traffic regulations allowed. He was a good driver, threading his way through all the short cuts. Anne, Dick, George and Timmy had all squeezed into the back of the car somehow, and Julian, being the largest, was in the front seat beside Thomas.

It seemed a long way, but at last they were there. Thomas drew up right outside Angela's bank, but on the other side of the road. The children had explained what it was all about on the way. Their plan was to follow Angela at a distance, and thus track down the anonymous letter-writer – or more likely, track down Mr Ernest Parry!

'I do hope Angela hasn't left the bank already!' said Anne anxiously.

But just then Angela herself appeared on the steps outside the door of the bank. She was carrying a bag which obviously contained the box with the pink pearls in it!

She hurried down the steps and started off along the pavement, walking fast and never looking behind her. The children could tell she was in a hurry to get it all over and done with.

'I thought she might take a taxi, but she hasn't,' said Dick.

'Which proves that the meeting place isn't far away,' George pointed out. 'Quick, let's get out and follow her on foot!'

The Five and Thomas all got out of the car. 'We'd better not stick together,' said Julian. 'She'll be more likely to notice us if you do. Thomas, you go first – Angela doesn't know you, so even if she turns round and sees you she won't suspect anything.'

Soon Angela turned right, into a particularly busy street. She seemed to hesitate for a moment, and then, just when the Five least expected it, she glanced over her shoulder. Thanks to Julian's bright idea, she saw no one but Thomas, and she had no reason to suspect *him*.

Obviously reassured, Angela went on along the street, walking fast. Then she slowed down. So did the children and Thomas. They all guessed the vital moment had come. Something was about to happen!

It was odd, though – so far as the Five could see, none of the passers by seemed interested in the young woman.

She slowed down even more. The children and Thomas got the impression she was looking out for something – or someone!

All of a sudden, Angela seemed to make up her

mind. The bag containing the box had been under her left arm – now she took it in her right hand, and quickly tossed it into a car which was parked by the pavement along which she was walking.

The window of the car was wound down, so it was easy. Angela just had to put out her arm, and the box fell in on the front seat.

It all happened in a split second. Unless you were watching really hard, you would never have noticed what Angela was doing, she moved so fast. She went on walking straight along the pavement as if nothing had happened. The children realized she must be following the instructions in the letter.

George let out an exclamation and rushed forward, followed by her cousins and the faithful Timmy. Thomas had already set off ahead of them, bounding past several surprised Christmas shoppers.

But it was too late!

The car, which had been standing there with its engine turning over, started off and moved away from the pavement. Thomas and George, both of them out of breath, came up with it at that very moment. They both tried to grab it – but all they did was scrape their fingernails on the bodywork.

Timmy tried snapping at the tyres, but that was no good either. The car went on its way, and was soon lost amidst the other traffic. Anne, following her brothers and her cousin, shouted, 'Stop it! Stop it!' As if that would be any good! Some of the people on the pavement laughed. They thought she was talking to Timmy, and in fact the dog was so angry to see his quarry get away that he was turning round and round in frantic circles!

However, Angela heard Anne's cry, and turned round. Seeing the Five, she exclaimed with surprise, and promptly retraced her steps.

'What on earth are you doing here?' she asked. 'How did you find me?'

George explained. Angela was white as a sheet.

'Oh, my goodness!' she murmured. 'You might have ruined everything.'

'No, we mightn't!' said Dick. 'We jolly nearly caught your horrible blackmailer. And if we had you'd have got your pearls back, and Monica would have had nothing to fear from him.'

'Well, at least my little girl is safe now!' sighed Angela.

'But the blackmailer's got away scot free,' said George, a little sharply.

'I ought to have followed Mrs Trevor in the car,' said Thomas ruefully. That reminded Julian that he ought to introduce Thomas to Angela, who seemed as if she was just waking from a nightmare. Now she was more herself again, she thanked them all, and patted Timmy. He was calming down at last!

'Please don't think me ungrateful!' she said. 'I know you meant it kindly, and I don't know how to thank you. You were trying so hard to protect me, but – well, never mind about the pearls now!

I hope that's the last I ever hear of the person who stole them.'

But the Five weren't giving up so easily. 'Did you see the face of the driver of the car?' Dick asked Angela.

'No, I didn't even turn my head – I'd been told not to.'

'And we arrived just too late!' said George, clenching her fists. She privately thought Angela had been rather weak, and she was cross with herself for not making better use of Thomas's car. She ought to have taken it into account that the writer of the threatening letter might come to the meeting-place by car himself!

Thomas very kindly offered to drive Angela home, and they all squeezed into the car. When they reached her flat they went up to say hallo to Monica, who had been left with one of the neighbours.

'And thank you all again!' said Angela gratefully. 'At least this strange business of my legacy and the stolen pearls has meant I got to know you children. I really do appreciate your friendship!'

When the Five said goodbye, Monica hugged her new friends – and Timmy put a stop to all this emotion by sneezing comically three times, one after another! Then the children left.

'I'll drive you home,' Thomas told them. 'What a shame we didn't bring it off! Just when I had a chance of sharing one of the Famous Five's adventures myself, too!'

'Our adventure isn't over yet!' said George, looking determined. 'I don't give up as easily as that, not when I've got an idea in my head – and my present idea is to bring Parry to justice!'

'Personally, I couldn't swear to it that he was the man who actually drove off with the pearls,' said Julian cautiously.

'It *is* him,' said George. 'I know he has the pearls – I *know* it! I'm so sure that I've made up my mind we'll get them back from him.'

'Get them back?' said Anne, sounding alarmed.

'Well, why not? I don't like to think of such a beastly man getting away with his crime right under our noses.'

George was really furious. Her cousins knew that when she lost her temper as badly as this it was hopeless trying to reason with her.

'What exactly did you think of doing next?' asked Dick.

'Well, for a start, I'd like to make sure Parry actually has the pearls,' said George.

'I thought that was what you *were* so sure of,' said Thomas, rather surprised.

'I am – that's not what I meant. I want to try and find out if Parry has the pearls at his own place, or if he's hidden them somewhere else.'

'Surely you're not going to walk straight into the lion's den?' said Thomas. 'Well, I must say, you certainly have plenty of nerve! Right, here we are, then,' he added, as they drew up outside their own block of flats. 'Don't hesitate to call on me if I can help you again – I'm entirely at your disposal. Goodbye for now, then!'

After lunch, the Five went out into the square gardens again. It was a sunny day, warm enough for them to sit on a seat in a sheltered corner, where they took stock of the situation.

'First of all we'd better keep watch on Mr Parry's shop,' said George. 'We'll try to find out about people he meets – at his own place or outside. And if necessary we must follow him. After all, he has to do *something* with those pearls if he wants to get hold of the money they're worth.'

'Hmm,' said Julian, thoughtfully. 'I don't know that keeping watch on the shop will get us anywhere much. Come on, George – if I know you, there's some other idea in your head as well! Out with it!'

'Oh, all right!' said George. 'I want to study the surroundings of the shop and the shop itself to see how we could get into it – openly or not!'

'What do you mean?'

'Well, we won't find out whether Parry has those pearls in his own keeping unless we actually go and look, will we?'

'But he knows what we look like now,' Dick pointed out. 'He'll chuck us out the moment we try setting foot in his shop. Anyway, what good would it do? I can't see myself saying, "How about giving me those pearls you stole from Mrs Trevor?" And even if I did, I can't see *him* saying, "Oh, certainly, since you ask so nicely, here they are!"'

George smiled. 'That's why I said openly or not! Come to think of it, I don't really see how we *can* get in openly. So since Parry broke into our sittingroom in the middle of the night, why don't we pay him back his own way?'

Julian frowned. 'No, George. That sort of thing's quite out of the question. You know perfectly well what Uncle Quentin and Aunt Fanny would say. They don't even like us being out by ourselves late at night in this big city, and they'd certainly want to know where we were going!'

'Don't get so worked up about it!' said George. 'This is something we'll have to discuss thoroughly before we go into action. But you're right – I don't think we could really get into the shop at night. I'm sure it's very well locked up. And we don't know whether Parry lives in a flat above the shop, or somewhere else. In fact we know very little about his habits – exactly what time the shop closes, and so on. So we must start by keeping a close watch on him, gathering all the information we can. *Then* we'll lay our plans.'

Even Julian could see no harm in just keeping watch on the shop. Dick and Anne agreed. So that was what the Five did over the next three days, standing guard in relays where they couldn't be seen from inside the shop itself. By the end of that time, they were ready to pool their information.

'Parry shuts at five in the evening,' Anne reported.

'He lives in a flat on the first floor,' Julian said.

'But he leaves the place about six to go and eat in a restaurant,' added Dick.

'He spends the time from five to six doing his accounts and making telephone calls, as far as we could tell from watching through the window,' said George. Then she summed up. 'Well, I've been thinking about it. And there's a simple but daring way we could bring our inquiries off successfully! This is what I thought we'd do . . .'

George's plan really *was* simple: she intended to get into the shop without being noticed before it was shut, hide somewhere, and not leave the place until she knew just where the pearls were hidden.

'You're part in it all is very important,' said George. 'I wouldn't feel safe without knowing you were all there to back me up. You'll know just where I am, and what risks I run if Parry happens to find me. If you don't see me come out again, you'll have to call the police. And since I'll know I'm covered, I shall be able to stand up to Parry if he happens to find me and tries threats or anything, all right?'

Julian, Dick and Anne saw all right – they saw George was determined to have her own way, never mind what risks she might be running! However, there was no arguing with George once she took an idea into her head . . .

The Five decided to go into action that very night.

8

Inside the Shop

A little before closing time, after making quite sure there were no customers left in the curio and souvenir shop, Julian opened the door and went in.

Dick, Anne and Timmy were already sheltering behind an advertisement hoarding only a few yards away from the shop. George was following Julian at a distance. When she saw her cousin go in, she stood outside the window, pretending to be looking at the things on display, but really watching what went on inside.

Julian walked towards Ernest Parry in a casual, offhand way. Parry's lips tightened. He obviously recognized his visitor. However, he didn't show it, and made himself smile.

'Good evening, young man. What can I do for you?' he asked.

Julian realized that the suspicious Parry wasn't going to take his eyes off him – which was exactly what he and George wanted! In fact, they were counting on it.

'Good evening,' he said politely. 'I wanted to buy my mother a little present. I saw you had some dried flowers made up into decorative shapes – could I have a closer look, please?'

Parry went over to a shelf that ran along one wall. Julian bent to look at the flowers at the same time as the shopkeeper, thus blocking his view of the door. This was the moment George had been waiting for!

Quickly and quietly, she slipped into the shop without being seen. Julian had left the door ajar as he came in, to make things easier for her. A few quick strides took George right across the shop and into the room behind it. Parry's back was turned to her as he watched Julian, and he never noticed her at all.

Once she was in the room behind the shop, George looked around. She had to find a hiding place at once. Of course, Julian would drag out the business of buying the dried flowers as long as possible, but there was no time to be lost.

The room where she found herself was quite large. A huge safe stood against the left-hand wall, and there was a divan by the wall at the back. A table and chairs stood in the middle of the room, and by the right-hand wall there was . . . 'Oh, good!' said George to herself. 'A big wardrobe! Just the place to hide!'

Even better, she saw that Parry's overcoat was hanging on the coatstand, so it wasn't very likely he would be opening the wardrobe, which seemed to have nothing but a raincoat hanging in it. Without a moment's hesitation, George got inside and pulled the door towards her, making sure she left it just ajar. Now all she had to do was wait.

Soon the sound of voices in the shop told her that Julian was paying for his flowers and leaving. She heard Parry bolt the shop door. It was closing time. Almost at once, he came into the room behind the shop. Peering through the gap in the wardrobe door, George saw him go over to the safe, open it, and take out a large notebook.

'That'll be his accounts book,' she said to herself.

Parry did not close the safe again, but went back into the shop. After three evenings of keeping watch, George knew just what he was doing now. He was sitting at his desk in the shop, checking the day's takings. Anyone walking past outside could see him doing his accounts -- he didn't usually pull down the old-fashioned metal shutter until he went out for his evening meal. And by then . . .

'By then I must have discovered whether the pink pearls are in that safe or not,' George told herself.

Well, this was her chance! George had never hoped that Ernest Parry would be kind enough to help her by leaving his safe open. But all the same, her heart was thudding at the thought of what she was about to do.

Very, very quietly, she pushed the wardrobe door open and came out of her hiding place. She made for the safe on tiptoe, straining her ears to hear any sound. Once she reached the safe she looked inside. There were boxes of various shapes in it, thick envelopes – and in one corner she saw a faded blue jewel box which looked very like the one containing the pink pearls. George put out her hand to make sure.

And then a creak stopped her! Ernest Parry's chair creaking! The shopkeeper had just risen to his feet – he must be coming back. George held her breath and hurried back into hiding. She was just in time. Parry came into the room and put his accounts book back, but he still didn't shut the safe. George saw him go back into the shop and then heard him pulling the metal shutter down.

That had been a close shave, though! She dared not come out of hiding again, open the door, and slip the contents into her pocket if it really *did* hold the pearls. She was afraid she wouldn't have time, and Parry would catch her in the act.

Sure enough, it wasn't long before he came back into the room once more. Peering through the crack in the door, George saw him go over to the safe again.

'Bother!' she thought to herself. 'He's sure to close it *this* time!'

But she was wrong. When Parry turned round, he was holding the box. He opened it with a gloating expression on his face, and before George's dazzled eyes he took out the double row of pink pearls, stroking them with his fingertips. It looked as if he couldn't take his eyes off them.

All of a sudden he was interrupted by the telephone ringing. He started, threw the pearls and then the box into the safe, and slammed the safe door shut. It closed with a distinct click.

'So there we are!' said George to herself, furiously. 'I've found the pearls all right, but I can't lay my hands on them!'

All she could do was wait – and listen to what Parry was saying over the phone.

'Oh, it's you, is it, Hatsumoto? What's the idea, calling at this time of day? I've only just shut up the shop. I might easily still have had a customer here, and then I couldn't have talked to you freely, could I? In future perhaps you'll be kind enough not to ring except at the times we agreed – it only needs one indiscreet move to sabotage the cleverest of plans . . . What? No, of course not! But we must be careful . . . What did you say? . . . You were anxious to know if I'd received the goods? Now listen to me, Hatsumoto! I trust this will be the last time you and your friends call me unexpectedly like this!'

There was silence while Parry listened to what his caller was saying at the other end of the line. Then he started talking again.

'You know quite well that if you want precise details about the arrival of each new consignment of pearls, you only have to pass my shop and look in the window. That means we can avoid conversations, by telephone or in person – they're always dangerous. Understand? Do I need to remind you what to do? When you see the goods have arrived, *then* you ring me, and you just ask, "How much?" And I'll tell you the price. After that, you know the next step, don't you? Money on delivery of the pearls. Right – goodbye!'

Parry hung up. In her hiding place, George was holding her breath. She had just realized that the shopkeeper was more than an occasional jewel thief – he ran a regular trade in pearls! Annoyed by his caller, he'd been talking too freely.

George had read somewhere that genuine Japanese pearls were among the most sought-after of all on the world market. But unfortunately they were very expensive, and carried very high Customs duties. Was it possible that Parry was a go-between dealing with illegal consignments of Japanese pearls and receivers of stolen goods who lived in England? George's head was whirling! The situation was a lot more dangerous than she had ever guessed it might be. George shivered in spite of herself, but then she plucked up courage again. 'I'll get out of this somehow!' she told herself.

After hanging up, Parry sat at his desk thinking for a moment. Then he came back into the room behind the shop, opened the safe door, put the pearls carefully back into their box and put the box back in its place, locked the heavy door and jumbled up the numbers of the combination.

Through the crack in the wardrobe door, George saw him put on his overcoat. That was a great relief! He was going out – and at last she'd be able to leave too. The others must be getting impatient, waiting outside.

A moment later, George heard the front door of the shop close behind him. Only then did she dare come out of hiding.

'Phew!' she breathed. 'To think Angela's pearls are here, behind that safe door. And there's nothing I can do about it this evening. All the same, I've found out even more than I expected. So now to find the others and tell them all about it. Won't they be surprised!'

Still moving carefully, George made her way to the back of the room behind the shop. She knew there was a small door there, behind the divan, opening on to a flight of steps which led down into a cellar where the shopkeeper kept his stock. The Five had been hard at work with their inquiries over the previous three days.

George had left nothing to chance. She had found out that the cellar was lit by a small window high up in its wall and looking out on the alleyway behind the buildings. The window wouldn't be big enough to let a grown-up through, but George was small and slight, and could climb out of it easily. Once she was in the cellar, she clambered on some old furniture standing there, hoisted herself up to the level of the window, looked to make sure the coast was clear – and soon she was outside, no worse for wear except for a tear in her jeans. She ran round the block to find her cousins and Dick, who were all delighted to see her.

'There you are at last!' said Dick. 'We were beginning to worry. What did you find out? Quick, tell us!'

George was happy to oblige – and on the way home, she breathlessly told them all about her adventure.

'Right – from what you say, George, we can conclude that Parry's not just a thief but a criminal running an illegal racket in pearls,' said Julian. 'It's obvious that he gets up to all sorts of shady business under cover of keeping his shop.'

'We must put a stop to it!' said Dick.

'I don't suppose that will be easy, though, will it?' Anne ventured to say. She was still feeling alarmed by the thought of all the risks George had been running.

'No, not easy, but not *impossible*,' said George. 'Thanks to that phone conversation I overheard between Parry and one of his accomplices, we now have an important clue!'

'What clue?' asked Dick.

'Well, somebody looking in Parry's shop window

is supposed to be able to tell from it whether the "goods" have arrived or not. So we must keep watching that window ourselves, and keep our eyes open for any change in the display.'

'Good idea, George,' said Julian approvingly, and the others thought so too. Even Timmy gave a 'Woof!' of approval.

So next morning the Five were on the trail again. Surrounded by a crowd of busy Christmas shoppers, they stared into Mr Parry's shop window. However, hard as they looked, they couldn't see anything suspicious about it. Dick had a bright idea, and took a photograph of the window display, so that they could check for any changes in it later.

Next day was Sunday. Uncle Quentin didn't have any meetings at his conference, but he and Aunt Fanny were going to visit some of Cousin Jane's friends. So, after Sunday lunch the children had the afternoon free to do as they pleased. 'Let's go to the city zoo!' suggested Julian. 'I've heard it's a good one.'

It *was* a good zoo – and the children were all enjoying themselves looking at the animals until suddenly, to their amazement, they caught sight of none other than Ernest Parry, standing on a gravel path not far from them. What a coincidence! He was deep in conversation with a Japanese man, and after a minute or so the Japanese man gave him a box.

'I say!' whispered George. 'That box is just like some that I saw at the back of his safe!'

'I think we'd better separate and follow both men,' Julian quickly decided.

But he hadn't reckoned with the mischievous chimpanzee in the cage nearby. Timmy had stopped rather close to the cage – and the chimp grabbed his tail through the bars and gave it a good tug! Poor Timmy yelped with pain, and started barking at the top of his voice. 'Woof! Woof!' A crowd gathered around the children, some of them laughing at Timmy, which of course made George furious. At last a keeper arrived on the scene, and with some difficulty persuaded the monkey to let go.

When all the noise and confusion had died down, the Five realized that Parry and the Japanese man were nowhere to be seen.

'What a shame!' sighed Dick. 'We might have found out something new.'

'Do you think that box had pearls in it?' asked Anne.

'It's quite possible,' said George, petting poor Timmy, who hadn't got over the undignified attack on his tail yet. 'Perhaps Sunday is the day they – er – deliver the goods.'

None of the children slept very well that night. They were wondering if Parry had really received a delivery of pearls. And next day, when they went to look at his shop in the afternoon, they felt sure he had! Even from a distance, they could see the window display had been changed. The shop was closed on Monday mornings, so obviously Parry had altered the display during the morning, behind his metal shutter. The children took shelter in the cover of the advertisement hoarding again, and Anne, who looked so sweet and harmless, was given the job of going to take a good look at the window. When she came back her face was pink with excitement.

'I compared it with Dick's photo,' she told the others, 'and the same things are there as before, but arranged in a different way – and there are some new things too.'

'What sort of new things?' George asked at once.

'They're all of them little boxes decorated with shells – you know, the sort of thing people buy as souvenirs of the seaside.'

'I know what you mean – they're hideous, if you ask me!' said Dick.

George was thinking. 'That sort of souvenir is very outdated now,' she said. 'I shouldn't have thought Parry would sell many – so why put them on show?'

'He could have bought them cheap from some-body's bankrupt stock,' suggested Julian. 'Oh – wait a minute. Look at that!'

The others looked – and peering round the hoarding where they had taken cover, they could see a small, thin man, walking slowly past Mr Parry's shop.

'He's Japanese!' whispered Dick. 'And now he's going in! Hang on a moment while I get my binoculars out!'

Dick put the binoculars to his eyes, and uttered a sudden exclamation.

'I say – Parry's taking one of those little boxes out of the window. The ones with shells on them, that Anne saw in there. Bother – it's too dark further inside the shop for me to see much more. Hang on – here comes the Japanese man out again, holding a package. It must be the box!'

'And did you notice, he had another package under his arm when he went in?' said George. 'A bigger one. He's not carrying it now.' She thought for a bit, frowning, and then said, 'If the shell souvenir box contains pearls, it's quite possible that the bigger parcel held money to pay for them, in cash. They could have done their business very fast, in that case, and even if there were any other customers in the shop, all they'd have noticed would be that somebody had left a package behind by mistake. Nothing odd about that!'

'But if it's money,' said Anne, 'wouldn't Parry have wanted to open the package and count it?'

'No, wolf doesn't eat wolf!' said George, remembering a proverb which seemed to fit the circumstances. 'I mean, they've got to be honest among themselves, if they want their racket to keep going smoothly.'

'Never mind all that – what do we do now?' asked Dick impatiently. 'We can hardly follow the Japanese man and snatch his box, can we? He may be perfectly innocent.'

'I suppose so,' said George. 'Well, let's go on watching the shop, to see what happens next.'

So the Five went on keeping watch. And they didn't regret it, because though there were quite a lot of genuine customers visiting the shop to buy Christmas presents, they saw three more 'suspects' going in and coming out again. Two Japanese and one European went into the shop carrying a package or a large envelope, and seemed to be buying one of the ugly boxes covered with shells. And when they came out, they had all left their original packages behind!

'That practically proves that they're up to some kind of shady business,' said George.

'*Practically* isn't the same thing as *completely*,' Julian pointed out, looking grave.

'All right, Ju, let's make sure we have some really solid evidence, then!' said George. 'That's what we need.'

'Yes, quite, but how are we going to get it?'

'I've thought of an idea, of course!' George told her cousin.

'Never!' said Dick. 'I suppose we might have known it!'

George took no notice. 'It's going to be Anne who does the reconnaissance this time.'

'Me?' said poor Anne. She didn't like the sound of that at all.

'Don't worry, you won't be running any risks,' said George. 'You see, it's more than likely Parry took less notice of you than any of the rest of us. Look!' And George rummaged in the bag that had once been used to carry Timmy. 'I *thought* this might come in useful! It's a black wig I found in the cupboard in our room – there are several of them there. I expect they're Cousin Jane's. I'm sure she wouldn't mind if we borrowed this one. Put it on, Anne, quick – there! You look completely different now. If by any chance Parry *did* notice you, he won't recognize you again. And you'd better wear these sunglasses to hide your blue eyes.'

'All right – what else do you want me to do, though?' asked Anne, not very enthusiastically.

'Just go into Parry's shop like any ordinary customer and say you want to buy one of those shell-covered boxes.'

'Are you sure that's all you're planning, George?' asked Julian, who was very protective towards his little sister.

'Yes, honestly, and I promise there isn't any danger! But it will be very interesting to see how Parry reacts. Of course, he may be quite happy to sell the box – '

'Hm – I must say, that would be rather disappointing!' said Julian, grinning despite himself.

'But then again, he may refuse to sell, and *then* we'll know for sure we're on the right track. Go on, Anne, and don't worry!' said George.

Anne certainly looked a different person in her black wig and dark glasses. She walked along the pavement towards the shop, and timidly opened the door. Parry was alone. When he saw a customer come in, he automatically smiled brightly.

'Yes, my dear, can I help you?'

Anne realized that he didn't recognize her, and that was a help. 'I wanted to buy a local souvenir,' she said, turning towards the window as if she wanted to choose something. 'Oh, aren't those little boxes all covered with shells sweet!'

'I'm afraid they're not for sale,' said the shopkeeper quickly. 'I only put them in the window as background for the display. How about something else? Look at these necklaces and bracelets – they're charming, and not at all expensive.'

'But I really *did* want one of those boxes,' said Anne, sounding disappointed. 'Are you sure they're not for sale?'

'Quite sure,' said Parry firmly, and Anne didn't insist. She knew he was lying! She looked at the other things, said there wasn't really anything she liked, and let Parry go to the door with her. He seemed in quite a hurry to get rid of his customer!

Anne had the sense to go all round the block in order to join George and her brothers, just in case Parry happened to be watching her.

'So he wouldn't sell!' cried the others, when she told them what had happened.

'And I was quite right!' added George, triumphantly. 'Well, let's hurry home. There's no time to be lost! My turn to borrow one of Cousin Jane's wigs now, and I hope all the boxes with shells on them won't be sold by the time I get back to the shop.'

Once they were home again, George told the others her plan.

'I thought I'd disguise myself and try buying one of those boxes too. I might discover something – no, *not* you, Timmy! You're not coming, I'm afraid. Not this time! You'd ruin my disguise! Just for once, you'll have to stay behind.'

And a little later George, equipped with a short auburn wig, a few false freckles and an American accent, was trying to buy a souvenir from Mr Parry.

9

The Secret of the Seashells

'Say, I want to buy a present for my sister back home in the States,' said George, sounding as American as possible. 'Do you have something nice?' As she spoke, she was looking at the window display. There were only two of the shell-covered boxes left now!

'All kinds of nice things, young man!' said Ernest Parry, with his oily smile. The auburn wig, short like George's own hair, didn't make any difference to her usual boyish look. Just as she had hoped, Parry had not recognized her. She pointed to one of the boxes.

'I'll take that box with the shells on it – it's real cute!' she said.

'Oh, I'm afraid that's not for sale,' said Mr Parry quickly.

George looked disappointed. 'Oh, what a shame. Maybe – '

But she was interrupted by a man who greeted Mr Parry and stood there waiting to be served.

Noticing the large envelope under his arm, George suspected this was another of Mr Parry's very special customers.

'Maybe I'll take the other box, then,' she said, pointing to the second shell-covered box in the window and raising her voice. Out of the corner of her eye, she could see the man who had just come in give a nervous start. Parry looked annoyed.

'I'm afraid neither of them is for sale, young man. Choose something else!'

In the end, George bought a small paperweight and left. No sooner had she walked a little way down the street, however, than she turned and retraced her steps. As she walked past the window, she saw that one of the boxes had gone. A moment later, Mr Parry's 'customer' came out of the shop holding a small package, and minus his big envelope. Parry, wearing a broad smile, had come to the doorway with him, so George hurried off for fear he might notice her.

She got back to the advertisement hoarding, where she had arranged to meet the others. They had decided on their movements before they parted, and George was anxious to know how Julian, Dick and Anne had got on.

They had been busy too! Leaving Timmy at home, much to the dog's disgust, they had gone to a nearby street market, where they knew there were several stalls of second-hand junk. It was Anne who found what they were looking for first. She called her brothers over.

'Look!' she said. 'A box covered with shells, very like the ones Mr Parry had in his window – and it looks almost new, too!'

'Good!' said Dick. 'Let's hurry up and buy it, and then go and meet George!'

They bought the box, and as it hadn't cost much, they decided to treat themselves to a taxi for the journey to Mimosa Avenue. When they got there, they found George waiting impatiently.

'Did you find one?' she asked as they got out of the taxi and Julian paid the driver. 'You're just in time – there's only one box left in the window now!'

'Don't worry, George, here's what we wanted!' said Julian proudly, producing the shell-covered box they had bought in the street market from a carrier bag.

George looked at it. 'Splendid!' she said. 'It's just like those hideous boxes that have been disappearing from Parry's window. Well – now for the second part of my plan!'

'Do be careful, George!' said Anne anxiously.

George put the box back into the carrier bag, and then marched off towards the curio and souvenir shop again. Her cousins watched her go.

She was determined to find out just what was in those shell-covered boxes, and her bold idea was to exchange the last one for the box her cousins had just bought.

She had chosen a good moment. Parry was busy helping two young women who were choosing costume jewellery and couldn't make up their minds. He saw the 'American boy' come into the shop out of the corner of his eye, but not realizing it was George, he saw no cause for alarm.

George made sure he wasn't watching her too closely, and then went over to the window and pretended to be looking at a row of little puppets on strings. Then, seizing her chance while Parry was giving his customers change, she quickly put out her arm, picked up the box in the window, and replaced it with the box from the carrier bag. Picking up one of the puppets – a clown – she went over to Parry.

'I guess I'll take this cute little puppet too,' she said, in her American accent. She paid for it, and hurried out – almost bumping into a well-dressed man in the doorway.

'I did it!' she told her cousins triumphantly. 'Here's the box! A minute or so more and I bet it would have been too late. Watch the shop window!'

Sure enough, they could make out Ernest Parry inside the shop as he went to the window and took out the last of the shell-covered boxes – the one George had left there.

George chuckled. 'Oh, I wish I could see the "customer's" face when he finds out what he's got! He isn't going to be a bit pleased with Mr Parry.'

Suddenly Anne had a very bold idea. 'Why don't we follow that man?' she said, pointing to the well-dressed customer who was just coming out of the shop. 'We might find out who he is – and then we'd have some facts about at least one of Parry's accomplices.'

'Well done, Anne! That's a very good idea,' said George approvingly. 'Come on, everyone!'

The children waited until the man was a little way off, and then started following him at a distance. After a while, they saw him go into one of the biggest jewellery shops in town. They stood outside the window, and saw him walk right through the shop and into the room behind it. He must be the jeweller himself.

'So now we know!' said Julian. 'Parry is selling illegally imported pearls – and some of them are bought by businesses that look as if they're perfectly honest! Well, that really is the limit!'

'All we have to do now is unmask him,' said Dick. 'The box George took out of his window ought to help us there.'

'I hope so,' agreed George. 'Quick, let's go home and look inside it.'

Timmy was delighted to see the children back, and jumped up at them, barking happily. He didn't like being left at home. There was still plenty of time before Aunt Fanny called them to come and have supper, so the Five all went into the boys' room. George took off her wig, and then put the box on the table. They all looked at it, hardly daring to lift the shell-covered lid.

'It's even uglier close to!' said Dick.

'All the same, it probably contains a fortune,' said Julian.

This was a solemn moment. 'Go on, George, open it!' Anne told her cousin.

However, Julian was gently shaking the box. 'I can't hear anything moving inside,' he said with some concern.

'Well, let's look!' said George. She undid the little clasp of the box, lifted the lid and — 'Oh!' gasped everyone.

'Woof!' barked Timmy, not wanting to be left out again.

The box was empty!

Had their deductions been wrong all the time? Had they been imagining things? George simply couldn't believe it.

'No!' she said out loud, answering the question they were all asking themselves. 'We can't have made a mistake like that! There *have* to be pearls hidden somewhere in this box.'

Anne felt inside it. It had a flimsy paper lining, and there were no suspicious lumps or bumps anywhere. It was just an ordinary box.

'Perhaps there's a false bottom?' suggested Julian.

Dick felt the bottom of the box — so hard that his finger broke right through the cardboard it was made of and came out the other side.

'No false bottom,' he said gloomily. 'No hiding place at all. Absolutely nothing! We've made a mistake. This is one time the Five *don't* come out on top!'

'Woof!' said Timmy, in a reproachful tone of voice.

But George had picked up the box and was looking closely at it.

'Hang on a moment!' she said. 'Suppose this box *does* have a secret hiding place, and it *isn't* at the bottom, then it must be in the lid or the sides.'

'They're too thin, George, just like the bottom of the box,' said Julian.

'Perhaps it's under the shells stuck on top?' Anne ventured to suggest.

'Now that's an idea!' said George. She borrowed Dick's penknife and slipped the blade gently underneath one of the shells. It was a curly whelk shell. Her cousins watched in suspense. But when she had prised it off, there was nothing on the lid of the box underneath it. Anne took the shell itself and shook it, but there was no rattling sound inside. She put it back on the table, disappointed.

'Try another,' said Dick, not very hopefully.

One by one, George prised off all the shells stuck to the lid of the box – and found nothing underneath them! The children sat there looking at the box, now just a cardboard framework with no mystery about it, and a little pile of shells beside it.

George was so disappointed that she lost her

temper, and flattened the cardboard box with her fist. 'So much for *that*!' she said angrily. 'And so much for these beastly shells, too!'

She swept them off the table, and they went bouncing away in all directions. Timmy thought it was a game, and his mistress had thrown the shells for him to catch. Bounding happily after them and wagging his tail, he caught a whelk shell in his mouth and cracked it as if it were a nut!

It didn't taste very nice, and Timmy was quick to spit it out again. He looked so funny, with an expression of disgust on his face as he looked at the bits of broken seashell, that the children couldn't help laughing.

And then, suddenly, George let out a cry. She bent down and picked up a small object lying on the carpet.

When she straightened up again, there was something shining in the palm of her hand.

'Look at that!' she said, awestruck.

'A pearl!' cried Anne. 'Oh, isn't it lovely!'

'Hurray!' cried Dick.

'I *say*!' exclaimed Julian. He took the pearl, which really was a magnificent specimen, and examined it. 'Look – it's still got a bit of the shell sticking to it. It was *glued* in place,' he said, showing the others. 'That must be why the shell Anne shook didn't rattle.'

Dick and George were already on all fours, retrieving the shells that had gone flying over the floor. Working very carefully, probing the inside of each shell with a toothpick, the children felt for anything that might be glued there and dislodged it. They ended up with twelve superb pearls!

'We did it!' they shouted.

'We've solved the mystery!'

'Down with Mr Parry!'

'I bet he ends up in jail!'

'Woof! Woof!' agreed Timmy.

All of a sudden the door was opened, and there stood Uncle Quentin, looking very cross. 'What on earth is going on?' he asked. 'What's the meaning of all this noise? I've only just come in, and you can be heard right out in the street!'

'Oh, Father!' cried George, letting Timmy go. 'Look – look what we've found!'

'We've – we've just solved a mystery, you see, Uncle Quentin,' Julian explained. 'It was all to do with these!' And he pointed to the table, where Anne had arranged the pearls in a neat line.

'Pearls, Uncle Quentin!' Dick helpfully explained.

'They *are* real, aren't they?' said Anne.

Staggered, Uncle Quentin looked at the beautiful pearls. 'This is incredible!' he said. 'Where did you find them ?'

'Well – it's rather a long story,' George began.

'Then you'd better tell us over supper,' said Uncle Quentin.

As the children might have expected, Aunt Fanny was horrified to think of the risks they had been running – and Uncle Quentin was inclined to scold them.

'All right, I know we should have told you, Father,' George admitted penitently. 'But you know how it is – we got carried away by the course of events. And anyway, we *have* solved the mystery of those Japanese pearls!'

'Yes, and we know where Angela Trevor's necklace is,' added Dick. 'So now all we have to do is tell the police, Uncle Quentin.'

Uncle Quentin did. He and the children went to the nearest police station straight after supper, and told the officers on duty there the whole story. As it was such a serious matter, *they* called the Superintendent at his home, even though it was quite late now, and he came to the police station at once to hear what Uncle Quentin and the children had to say.

The Superintendent took charge of the precious pearls, and said, 'Well, we'll be acting on this information tomorrow. We'll get a search warrant for Parry's shop, and arrest him. I hope that then he'll agree to name his accomplices.'

Uncle Quentin and the children went home again – by now they were feeling rather tired. But before they went to bed, George asked her father, 'Do you think we can go too when the police search Parry's shop tomorrow?'

'No, I don't,' said Uncle Quentin. 'The police won't want you getting in their way.'

George said no more – but she was determined that they *would* be there, somehow or other, when the police arrested the man the Five had unmasked.

'We want to be sure he doesn't slip through the fingers of the police,' she told her cousins. 'He's so cunning, he might try something.'

'I know – let's ask Thomas if he'd like to come with us!' said Dick. 'I'm sure he'd be interested – and he could drive us, too,' he added, looking on the practical side.

Thomas was fascinated to hear the story when they telephoned him early next morning, and said he'd be happy to borrow his father's car and drive them to Mimosa Avenue. They arrived in good time, just as the shops were opening, and parked opposite the souvenir shop, waiting in silence for the police to arrive. Soon they saw two plainclothes men get out of a black car. A police car drew up behind it. The two men walked towards the shop.

'Plain-clothes detectives,' murmured Thomas. 'They'll be here to search the place and take Parry away.'

'I don't suppose we'll see much from here,' said Dick, disappointed.

'Wait a minute!' said George. 'I've got an idea. Follow me!'

Thomas locked the car, and they all went after George as she swiftly made her way round the block. As they hurried along, she explained, 'That alley behind the shops here is almost always deserted.

We can get into Parry's cellar through the window high up in its wall. There'll still be a locked door between us and the room at the back of the shop – but even if we can't see anything, we'll be able to *hear* what's going on.'

They made their way through the little window – even Thomas, who luckily was thin and athletic – and stood as close as they could to the locked door of the cellar. From here, they could hear quite distinctly as one of the police officers told Parry, 'Now then, open that safe!' And a few minutes later, the same voice said, 'Aha! So here are the pink pearls that were stolen from Mrs Trevor!'

'Take a look at these boxes,' said the other officer. 'More pearls! I don't suppose you can show us the receipted invoices for these, can you, Parry? No, I rather thought not! Well, you'd better come with us!'

George and the others exchanged triumphant glances. The police had found the evidence all right, and Parry was being taken away.

'Hurray!' said Dick. 'They're arresting him – he won't be able to do any more harm!'

The Five and Thomas left the cellar the same way as they had come – but there was still a surprise in store for them! As they came out of the alley and into Mimosa Avenue again, they saw Parry rush out of his shop. He was not wearing handcuffs, there were no policemen with him, and he was obviously in a tearing hurry!

They realized that he must have resisted arrest, because his clothes were in a state of disorder – and he was holding the blue box which contained the pink pearl necklace. There was an expression of ferocious determination on his face.

'He's escaped!' cried Anne in alarm.

'Not yet, he hasn't!' said George.

Now the two plain-clothes policmen emerged from the shop in their turn. One of them was bleeding from the nose, and the other was waving his arms about. 'Stop that man!' he shouted, shaking his fist at Parry who dashed across the road, obviously meaning to lose himself in the crowd of Christmas shoppers and people hurrying to work on the other side.

Uniformed policemen were already getting out of the parked police car. 'I don't think they're going to be in time,' said Julian.

'Stop him!' shouted the plain-clothes man again.

'With pleasure!' said George, and turning to Timmy she told him, 'Go on, Timmy, get him! Good dog! Get him – bring him back here! Quick!'

Timmy was very quick to understand George's orders. Before the astonished eyes of all the policemen, Timmy leaped away across the road, in pursuit of Parry. Car tyres squealed as drivers braked hard. 'That dog nearly caused an accident!' shouted one man, winding down his car window.

George took no notice – she knew how clever and careful Timmy was, even when he moved fast. Sure enough, he easily avoided all the cars, and was soon on the other side of the road. He pounced on the fugitive just as Parry was getting into a passing taxi he had hailed.

Then everything happened very fast. The policemen were shouting and blowing whistles. The taxi driver didn't know what had hit him as Timmy cornered his prey inside the taxi itself. When George, her cousins and Thomas arrived on the scene, they found Parry crouching on the seat, with Timmy keeping a firm grip on his coat.

'That's enough of that, Parry!' said one of the plain-clothes men, putting handcuffs on him. 'Well, done, children!' he added, turning to the Five. 'But for you, and this brave dog, we might have lost him!'

Next moment Parry was being taken off to the police station, and whatever awaited him there. He'd be spending Christmas behind bars!

Not surprisingly, there were newspaper reporters ringing up and calling at Cousin Jane's flat all afternoon. The story of the pink pearl necklace and the illegally imported Japanese pearls was splashed all over next morning's front pages, along with a photograph of the children – and Timmy too, of course. 'Another Adventure of the Famous Five!' said one of the newspapers, giving a full report of the arrest of Ernest Parry.

Angela Trevor and Monica were in the papers too. Aunt Fanny invited them both to spend Christmas

Day, which was now only a day or so away, with herself and Uncle Quentin and the children, and it was a very happy Christmas for everyone! Even Uncle Quentin didn't seem to mind too much that this scientific conference was taking a break for a few days.

The conference went on for another week after Christmas, and then it was time to go home to Kirrin Cottage. The Five went to see Angela to say goodbye, and their new friend Thomas kindly borrowed his father's car again and drove them to her flat for tea.

She was delighted to see them. 'I shall never be able to thank you enough for all the risks you ran to get back my necklace!' she said. 'I have no fears of the future for myself and Monica now, thanks to the money I'm getting from the sale of the pink pearls. You have no idea what a relief that is!'

She still had some questions to ask about Parry and his activities, and the children, who had heard all about it from the police, told her what they knew as they ate the delicious tea she had ready for them.

'Parry has confessed everything and given the police the names of his contacts and accomplices,' said Julian. 'They're all behind bars now. It seems that our friend was really just an intermediary between the people who were buying and selling those illegally imported Japanese pearls.'

'So really, the business of your necklace was only

a sideline to him!' said George. 'He learned of its existence only by chance.'

'How was that?' asked Angela, pouring more tea and passing a plate of squidgy chocolate cake round.

'Well, you see, Parry's grandmother was a friend of old Miss Longfield's,' George explained. 'It was when his grandmother died, and he was looking through some letters from her friends he found in her desk, that he discovered the facts about the pink pearls – *and* the place where Miss Longfield used to hide them when she went out, down between the seat and the back of her old tub chair! So you can imagine how he felt when he knew the contents of her flat were going to be sold at auction. He went to look at the furniture when it was on view the day before the sale – we got there with my mother a moment later, just as he had slipped his hand down into the hiding place, and felt that the box was there. But he couldn't take it out with so many people looking at him! However, that was why he tried to buy the chair from my mother when she had been bidding for it successfully at the sale. He was determined to have it, so when she wouldn't sell, he tried to burgle us and steal it. And you know the rest of the story.'

'But how did Parry find out about *me*?' asked Angela.

'By following us, I'm afraid,' said Julian. 'We ought to have been more careful.'

'Are you really going away?' Monica asked George, patting Timmy.

'Yes, we have to go home,' George told the little girl. 'But we'll come back and see you one of these days.'

And then it was time for the Five to go back to Cousin Jane's flat and pack for the journey home to Kirrin next day. How glad they were to think of Parry and his accomplices safe in prison!

'What exciting holidays these have been,' said George, as they got on the train to London. 'And what an exciting adventure! Do you think we'll be having any more adventures soon, Timmy?'

'Woof!' said Timmy. 'Woof!'

If you liked this book by Claude Voilier, you are certain to enjoy the original Famous Five stories by Enid Blyton. These are published by Hodder Children's Books: